When Lightning Strikes

Shouldering the reputation of a lethal gunfighter has its downsides, as Lightning Cal Gentry soon discovers. Brash hotheads who think they have the edge are always eager to make their play. Hard-cases think that being a fast gun brings respect and fame – not to mention the girls and free drink.

Cal knows from experience that it's easier to gain your place at the top than to stay there – and now he wants out. But shucking such a dubious state is more difficult to achieve than he ever imagined.

When he guns down Billy Vance in the New Mexico town of Tucumcari, the act heralds the start of a manhunt that puts his loved ones in mortal danger. Only with the help of the infamous renegade Apache, Geronimo, can he hope to resolve the issue.

When Lightning Strikes

Ethan Flagg

A Black Horse Western

ROBERT HALE · LONDON

© Ethan Flagg 2011
First published in Great Britain 2011

ISBN 978-0-7090-9087-8

Robert Hale Limited
Clerkenwell House
Clerkenwell Green
London EC1R 0HT

www.halebooks.com

The right of Ethan Flagg to be identified as
author of this work has been asserted by him
in accordance with the Copyright, Designs and
Patents Act 1988

Typeset by
Derek Doyle & Associates, Shaw Heath
Printed and bound in Great Britain by
CPI Antony Rowe, Chippenham and Eastbourne

ONE

TUCUMCARI

Cal Gentry drew his mount to a halt on the edge of the town. Quietly and with a practiced eye he surveyed the single street of adobe buildings. Nothing moved. The orange and red flag of New Mexico hung listless and somewhat dejected in the fetid air.

Nailed to its pole was a faded sign informing travellers that they were about to enter the designated limits of Tucumcari which had a population of 376.

The small town simmered in the hot afternoon sun. Once a sentinel outpost for the Commanches who roamed these arid plains, the name translates as *lookout* in their tongue. Cal's hard mouth crinkled. He much preferred the story told by an old Apache chief called Wautonamah who lived on the nearby mountain with his beautiful daughter, Kari.

Legend purports that two braves were selected as prospective husbands for the girl. The most accom-

5

plished would become head of the tribe. Kari had no say in the matter even though she hated the arrogant Tonapon. Her love was reserved for the second choice, Tocom.

The chief suggested a duel with daggers to decide the issue.

Kari overheard the tribal council's decision and hid in the trees to watch the outcome. When Tocom was slain by his adversary, she rushed out and stabbed Tonapon to death. The fallen brave fell across the body of Tocom. On hearing the news, the chief killed himself with the dagger crying, 'Tocum-Kari!' And the name stuck.

By the year of 1881, most of the warlike tribes had been confined to the reservations. And, Cal mused, they would hopefully remain there.

The dust-caked rider gave a nod of satisfaction noting that the main street was deserted. All he wanted was a place to rest up for a while and slake his thirst, maybe enjoy a hot meal before continuing his journey.

Tucumcari certainly appeared far too sleepy and lethargic to pose him any trouble. The last thing Cal Gentry needed was some hot-headed kid wanting to make a name for himself. Many had tried, but the gunfighter was still in the land of the living.

How many was it now? He had lost count after the number went into double figures.

A dark shadow clouded the lean face hidden beneath the wide brim of his battered Stetson. He felt drained, wearied of all the killing, of having to go up against gun-hungry tearaways whose sole ambition was to secure a reputation.

To be the one who gunned down Lightning Cal Gentry.

He shook his head. At thirty-five, he ought to be raising cattle on his own spread supported by a loving wife and family, not slinking about wondering where the next bullet was coming from. And many had found their mark: Cal had the scars to prove it.

Gingerly he fingered the latest addition. The red mark creasing his left arm still felt tender to the touch. That had been an unlucky meeting with some rustlers a week before while he was passing through the Oklahoma Panhandle. They had objected to his unwitting interruption to their cross branding. Cal had been lucky to get out alive.

For a change it was nothing to do with his having earned the questionable reputation of being a fast gun. And the more success he gained from defending that dubious honour, the greater became the myth that he was unbeatable.

It was a vicious circle that could only end one way. Boot Hill was littered with such luminaries – men who lived by the gun and thought they were invincible. Cal Gentry had no false illusions concerning his risky way of life. That was the reason behind his decision to head further west where he hoped to bury his past and start afresh.

It had all started accidentally.

Just a flukish encounter on the main street of

Bannock, Missouri near where his father had eked a precarious living from the land assisted by his two sons. Steve, the elder by three years, was content with the back-breaking toil of a dirt farmer, but Calvin balked at the very notion of such an existence.

There had to be easier, more exciting ways of making money.

He was ambling down the boardwalk one afternoon when two men ran out of the assay office clutching a sack. Both were toting hardware.

Even to a greenhorn it would have been obvious that a robbery had just taken place. Without thinking, Cal palmed his .36 Whitney and shot the first man. The guy was dead before his body hit the ground, a neat hole drilled in the centre of his forehead. The other outlaw turned, his own gun rising to the challenge.

Cal thumbed back the hammer. A burst of orange flame spat from the barrel. The robber spun in a tight circle clutching at his shattered hand.

The gunfire quickly attracted a host of curious onlookers – anything to relieve the monotony of everyday life. And the spilling of someone else's blood always offers an irresistible lure.

'Man, that sure was some kinda shooting,' observed one awestruck voice.

'The kid sure ain't no tenderfoot with that six shooter,' from another equally impressed bystander.

'What's happened here?' snapped the gruff voice of Morg Fender. The marshal elbowed a path through the swaying throng. 'Give me some room.'

'The assay office has been robbed and this fella stopped the critters in their tracks,' said the bartender of the local saloon still holding the glass he had been polishing.

Fender toed the still body of the deceased robber before turning his attention to the moaning figure huddled over his bleeding hand.

'Somebody get the doc while I jail this varmint,' boomed the marshal roughly hauling the twittering outlaw to his feet. 'And I'll need to hear your side of what happened,' Fender said to the rather bemused farmer.

'Classiest piece of gunplay I ever did see,' interjected the assay agent. 'Come and see me when you've given your statement to the marshal, kid. There'll be a reward in it for you.'

Cal was stunned into silence by all the attention he was receiving. Nonetheless, it was welcome. Seemed like that practice he had put in behind the old barn had paid off. Tin cans and bottles together with the odd rabbit for the stew pot were one thing; this was his first real bit of gunplay.

And his reactions had been swift and lethal. It felt good. These people were treating him like a hero, not some dumb nester on the scrounge.

'Drinks are on the house, Cal,' smiled the bartender slapping him on the back while ushering the startled youth towards the Lucky Strike Saloon. He was followed through the batwings by the bustling crowd of well-wishers all hoping that the free drinks would extend to them.

9

But it was the poignant comment of one old timer that sealed Cal Gentry's fate for years to come.

'That was one lightning fast draw, mister.' The stirring remark drew nods of approval from the surrounding mass. 'Ain't seen a smoother reaction since Hickok took out Dave Tutt in Springfield.'

Cal's eyes lit up. To be compared to the legendary Wild Bill was praise of the highest order.

'You got yourself a nickname, young man,' commented the barman. 'Lightning Cal Gentry.' A raucous cheer erupted as hats were thrown into the air.

Lightning Cal Gentry!

The appendage slipped off the tongue like an ice cream soda. Cal was in a dream as the first of many drinks slid down his throat.

It was late into the night before he left Bannock for the five mile ride back to the farm. Somehow he managed to stay on his horse. His life had changed forever. Calvin Gentry, the grubby, down-at-heel dirt farmer who had come to town earlier was no more. In his place was the boldly cocksure gunfighter reborn as Lightning Cal Gentry. He fingered the six-gun on his hip.

Nobody would look down their snooty noses at him ever again. He patted the rosewood pistol butt, a leery smile crossing the young face. Otherwise they'd have this fella to deal with.

It was on the following day after he had recovered from the celebratory drinking session that he remembered talk of a reward being offered. His father would be occupied in the north maize field all day and Steve was busy mending the barn roof. Lightning Cal would not be missed.

Before riding to Bannock he called on his buddy to accompany him. Tugg Miller was less impressed with Cal's prowess with a gun, reckoning himself on an equal footing. He was more concerned that his sidekick would share the reward. Both men had vowed that the first bit of serious money they earned would be spent on two classy dames from the Red Windmill Cathouse.

'You sure that mean-eyed critter in the assay office promised you a reward?' enquired a sceptical Tugg Miller for the third time. 'That skunk never gave anything away in his life unless there was some'n in it for him.'

'For the last time,' sighed Cal. 'I saved his dough, didn't I? That should be worth at least a hundred bucks.'

Tugg's eyes widened as his jaw hit the saddle horn. Lurid thoughts of the luscious bedroom delights to be enjoyed filled his swimming mind.

They drew up outside the assay office, stepped down and sauntered up to the door. A sharp rap brought a curt behest to enter. The two young men smiled at each other before smoothing down their rumpled Sunday suits. Hats clutched in their hands, they nervously entered the hallowed portal.

'Yes, boys,' asked the impatient agent offering the visitors a cursory glance. 'What can I do for you?'

Cal frowned. Surely the guy remembered his brave

action of the previous day. 'It's about the reward, Mister Rainham.'

Josh Rainham looked up from the ledger in which he was busy scribbling.

'Reward?' A blank look suffused the agent's blotched face.

'For checkmating those robbers yesterday,' pressed the perplexed hero. 'You promised me a reward.'

Rainham scratched his bald pate, suddenly appearing to recall what he now considered to be a somewhat rash announcement.

'Well, erm . . .' he blustered trying to think of some way to escape handing out any greenbacks. 'That was a fine thing you did, Calvin. But you should have left things to the marshal. After all, that's his job.'

Cal was less prone to a firey temper than his partner who quickly latched on to the fact that the sneaky toad was attempting to backtrack.

'Don't try no shifty stunts with us, mister,' snapped the waspish Miller. 'You know darned well what was said. Now pay up!'

'No need for that kind of talk, boys,' replied the agent in a placatory whine. 'Sure I remember. And here it is.' He reached into a pocket and withdrew a ten dollar bill.

Open mouths greeted the derisory offering.

'What you trying to pull, Rainham?' snarled the irate Miller. 'My buddy here saving your dough is worth a heap more'n that.' An angry finger jabbed at the crumpled note. 'I'd say you'd better think again, and quick before things turn nasty.'

Cal sensed that what had started off as an exciting prospect was rapidly escalating out of control. Deep down, however, he knew that his buddy was right: this smarmy dude was trying to welch on his undertaking. Normally calm and unruffled, Cal was fully caught up in the tense mood of indignation now dominating the stand-off.

'Now are you going to pay Cal here a proper reward?'

The agent scowled at the indignant farmhand.

'That's all you're getting from me,' he rasped pushing the note forward. 'Take it or leave it.'

It was not the right answer. They had reached the point of no return: a showdown was inevitable.

'We'll take a sight more'n a measly ten bucks,' growled Tugg Miller.

Rainham's hand slid beneath the counter to where he always kept a loaded shotgun. Cal saw the sly manoeuvre. He snatched the old Whitney from its holster and thumbed back the hammer.

'Leave it, mister. You're covered.'

A disdainful chortle issued from Rainham's leering mouth.

'Put it away, kid,' he guffawed scornfully eyeing the old weapon heavily scored with rust. 'Before someone gets hurt.'

That was the last straw for Tugg Miller. Without thinking he hauled out his own piece and shot the assay agent plumb through the heart. A look of total surprise drifted over the bloodless countenance as the assay agent slid from view behind the counter.

'Now you've really gone and upset the applecart,' opined a horrified Cal Gentry. 'What we gonna do?'

But Miller was unrepentent. 'Serves the greedy varmint right,' he leered, leaning over the counter to open a drawer. 'This'll pay for all the trouble he's caused.'

'Must be at least two hundred in there,' grinned Cal as the crazed fervour of the moment grabbed him in a steely embrace. He stuffed half the proceeds of the unexpected bonus into his coat pocket. 'Let's skidaddle before the law comes a-calling. That shot is bound to attract some unwelcome attention.'

The two greenhorn robbers dashed outside and leapt on their horses.

'Hold it you two!' hollered the marshal running down the street. A couple of shots buzzing past his ear encouraged the lawman to seek cover.

Once out of town, the pair of fugitives galloped off, only stopping to rest their mounts when they felt safe from pursuit. Only then did the true significance of what had so recently occurred strike home.

'You know what this means, buddy?' Miller postulated, a grave expression masking his youthful visage.

'Sure do, pard. We're big bad outlaws on the run,' replied Cal grinning from ear to ear. The euphoria of the moment was still coursing through his veins. 'And it feels a sight better'n slaving away on some dirt farm for the rest of my life.'

The only black spot was being wanted for a killing

he would much rather have avoided. But there was no turning back now. The past was behind him as the future beckoned.

'Yahooooo to that, partner!' hallooed Miller. 'Where we going from here?'

'They say there's a lot of action just waiting for enterprising guys like us in Kansas,' suggested Cal. 'Places like Abilene and Hayes City at the end of the cattle trails from Texas.'

'Then what we hanging around here for?'

Miller dug his spurs into his mount's flank. The startled animal leapt forward. It was followed by Lightning Cal Gentry as the pair of desperadoes headed west towards the state line.

TWO

THE TRUTH
WILL OUT

Cal hunched over the neck of his mount. Deftly he
built himself a quirly while continuing to survey the
deserted street. Satisfied with the probing appraisal,
he blew a gentle waft of air into the paint's left ear.

'Think we can have us a trouble-free stay in this
here burg, gal?' he murmured. The horse snickered
then stamped her right hoof. 'Yeh!' agreed Cal. 'Sure
looks that way.'

He nudged the paint back into motion.

His first stop was the livery barn where he handed
over a dollar for a spotty-faced youngster to grain and
water his tired cayuse.

'Any chance of getting a half decent meal in this
place?' he inquired, handing the reins to the young
man.

'The Chuckaluck does a fine chilli,' opined the ostler with enthusiasm. 'Tell the barman that Chip Sawyer recommended you. He'll see you right.'

Cal smiled to himself. Nothing like a bit of mutual help to oil the wheels of commerce. No doubt the 'keep sent passing travellers down here to have their mounts attended to.

'I'll do that, Chip,' he grinned walking off up the street. 'You just make sure the paint gets equal treatment.'

'Sure thing, Mister. . . ?'

'The name is. . . .' Cal paused. He was hoping that his reputation would not have spread this far west. But it always paid to err on the side of caution. 'Just call me Will Bennett.'

Shouldering through the door of the saloon, Cal sauntered over to the bar and ordered a large beer.

'Fella named Chip down at the livery said you do a mean chilli,' Cal said addressing the dapper looking bartender.

But he didn't receive the expected response. A broad smile spread across the guy's florid cheeks, his waxed moustache twitching.

'Sure we do, Cal. Best in town.' Then he hurried on. 'Remember me, buddy?' he gushed waving away the proferred payment for the drink. 'The name's Mel Tewksbury. I worked the bar of the Painted Lady in Witchita. You and Tug Miller were regulars until that incident with the travelling gambler.'

Cal stiffened.

That had been six years ago. Monty Dukes was the

gambler's handle, a shifty weasel who sported a flashy vest and beaverskin top hat. An ace of diamonds stuck in the silk hatband overtly advertised his profession. Cal was no expert poker player but he could recognize a cardsharp from fifty paces. And one was now sitting opposite at the green baize table.

The pot grew steadily until the guy made his final call. Only the two of them were left in the game. A crowd of eager voyeurs had gathered to find out who would walk away with the biggest pot in living memory.

'A full house, kings on eights,' grinned the preening tinhorn reaching for the heavy wad of greenbacks littering the table. 'Beat that!'

'Not so fast,' hissed Cal laying a restraining hand on the pile. 'Perhaps these gentlemen would like to see where that last king originated.' A steely grey peeper skewered the cocky gambler to the spot. Quick as a flash, Cal flipped the guy's jacket sleeve up to reveal an intricate mechanism designed to supply hidden cards.

'Well, well!' he declared, 'Now what have we here?' The purring tone of the accuser sounded all the more menacing in the hushed smokey atmosphere of the saloon.

'A dirty stinking card cheat!' snarled Miller slapping leather.

But Dukes was too fast. A small up-and-over Derringer concealed up his other sleeve appeared in his left hand. Both shots took Cal's hovering buddy in the guts. At the same time, the gambler kicked over the table. Drinks, cards and dough flew everywhere as he palmed a Colt Lightning from a shoulder holster.

Cal threw himself to one side, his own revolver instantly spitting lead. Three neatly placed shots perforated the gambler's chest before the varmint could get off a single shot. Blood oozed from the fatal wounds. He was dead before his bullet riddled body hit the floor.

A gasp went up from the ogling patrons of the Painted Lady as they emerged from cover. This was shooting well above the normal.

'That tinhorn should have known better than to cheat on Lightning Cal Gentry,' observed one awestruck spectator.

'He learned the hard way,' replied his partner as all eyes shifted to the young gunfighter.

'Gather up your dough, boys,' Cal said to the other card players who had been in the game. 'This guy can buy us all a drink with. . . .' He paused allowing a loose smile to crack the handsome visage, 'with his winnings!'

A cheer went up as everyone hustled over to the bar.

However, Cal was more concerned for his buddy. Miller was bleeding badly from the gutshot. A doctor was urgently summoned, but it was too late. Tugg Miller died in his friend's arms on the grubby floor of the Witchita saloon. His quick temper had finally gotten the better of him while the infamous reputation of Cal Gentry had been further enhanced.

Cal shook off the painful recall as he stared at his reflection in the mirror behind the bar. Five days' stubble concealed the grizzled leathery features. He was no longer a young man; streaks of grey in his hair and moustache gave him a tired, somewhat forlorn cast that was accentuated by the infamous notoriety he now carried.

It was a heavy burden that he would do anything to abandon.

Maybe once he reached Socorro, that finale could be achieved.

It was a bitter pill to swallow knowing that his reputation had filtered this far west. Maybe he could never throw off the heavy burden.

And now the telegraph was established in most settlements, that chance was fast diminishing. Barmen were like elephants – they never forgot, not to mention being notorious gossips. And they had the uncanny knack of being able to recall a face, especially one as infamous as that belonging to Lightning Cal Gentry.

It seemed that his name had become a byword far beyond the limits of Kansas and Missouri. There was only one way to nip this in the bud. Quickly recovering from the shock, he vehemently denied the association.

'You got the wrong fella, mister,' he stressed firmly.

The barman shook his head vigorously. 'No way,' he insisted. 'I never forget a name or a face. You're Lightning Cal Gentry.'

Cal's face hardened. Hooded eyes narrowed to

thin slits. This critter needed squashing urgently. His voice lowered to a tight-lipped growl, a sibilant whisper that was all the more forceful when delivered with a clenched fist thudding on the bar top.

'And I'm telling you that my name is Will Bennett,' snarled the gunfighter. 'I don't know you and I ain't never been anywhere near Witchita. Savvy?'

Tewksbury gulped.

'S-sure, if you say so, Mister . . . B-Bennett,' stammered the nervous barkeep hurriedly dispersing to the far end of the bar. From a safe distance he continued polishing glasses eyeing the newcomer with muffled suspicion. If that guy ain't the infamous gun-slinger known as Cal Gentry, then Mel Tewksbury would renounce his Irish ancestry.

Keeping a wary eye on the morose stranger, the doubting barman walked over to a group of card players in the corner who had signalled for him to bring over a fresh bottle.

'What was all that about, Mel?' enquired a heavy-set range hand grabbing hold of the bottle and topping up the glasses of the four players. 'Seemed like you were having words with that guy.'

Tewksbury shook his head, frustration etched across the florid countenance.

'I could have sworn blind that I knew him from Witchita,' muttered the barman casting surreptitious glances at the hunched drinker. 'When I asked him, he got all huffy, and denied it.' Tewksbury scratched his bald pate. 'But I never forget a face.'

'Who is he then?' pressed a young cocksure guy clad in a black vest and matching Stetson. Billy Vance was a known hothead around Tucumcari who liked to show off. 'You gonna let us in on the secret, Mel?'

The barman sucked in a deep breath before replying.

'Calls hisself Will Bennett.' Mel Tewksbury emitted a disdainful snort. 'But if that ain't Lightning Cal Gentry, I'm a green-eyed leprechaun,' expostulated the Irish bartender.

The four card players sat up, eyes agape and drilling into the back of the notorious gunfighter.

'You sure of that?' whispered a stupified little man adjusting his spectacles for a better look at the famous visitor.

Tewksbury had regained his composure.

'Ain't no doubt about it, boys,' he averred forcefully. 'Sure as eggs is eggs, that guy standing over there is Cal Gentry.'

Vance slowly pushed his chair back. Hitching up his tooled leather gunbelt with the new nickel-plated .45 he had recently purchased, the boy set his hat straight. This was his big chance. The opportunity to come out from under the shadow of his older brothers, show them he was a man, who deserved the respect of his peers.

'Hold it, Billy!' cautioned the older man at the table. Doc Standish enjoyed a drink and a game with the best of them. But, as with his poker playing, he displayed a cautious streak. 'You know who that is? They say he's killed over twenty men. And I don't want to be signing your death certificate afore the due time.'

'I heard it was thirty,' cut in the ranch hand called Chuck Raisin.

'Depends who's telling the tale,' returned the wary medic. 'They don't call him Lightning for nothing.'

'I saw Wyatt Earp gun down Bronco Fraser in Abilene,' the cowpoke iterated with huff. 'Ain't never seen a faster draw.'

Doc Standish jabbed a casual thumb towards the unsuspecting drinker at the bar. 'This guy would make Earp look like a tortoise.'

All eyes turned towards the awesome legend. Only Billy Vance remained aloof from the deferential glances.

The kid's thin lip twisted into a mocking sneer of contempt.

'He don't look so tough to me,' Vance scowled squaring his narrow shoulders. 'Ain't he just got two hands and two legs like any other fella?'

'Eugene won't be too pleased if'n he knows you've been tangling with Cal Gentry,' proferred the bank clerk.

That remark was like a red rag to a bull as far as Billy Vance was concerned. His mind was made up. Ever since his parents succumbed to the cholera epidemic of '77, the elder Vance had always treated Billy like a no-account kid.

That was about to change.

'Just gonna talk to the guy,' he replied lifting his shoulders. 'What's the harm in that?'

Then he moved across to the bar.

'Any chance of a drink up here?' called Vance trying to inject a mean slant into the curt demand. 'Or does our friend here get preferential treatment.'

Tewksbury hurried across to the strutting trouble-maker.

'Keep your voice down, Billy,' cautioned the nervous bartender. 'Didn't I just tell yuh who this was?'

'I just wanna talk to a big time gunfighter. Find out if'n he's human after all.' Vance then addressed Cal. 'How's about you and me have a drink together, Mister *Lightning* Gentry?' The kid laid a deliberately acerbic stress on to the nickname.

Cal sighed. He knew what was coming. This was how it always began. Some tearaway flexing his muscles trying to goad the renowned gunslinger into a fight. He remained silent turning away from the hovering roughneck. But that only served to exascer-bate the confrontation.

'That ain't no way to treat a fella who just wants to be friendly,' wheedled the kid. 'We like good manners here in Tucumcari. And that means accepting a drink from an open-handed stranger. Turning your back is just blamed insulting.' Vance hawked up a lump of phlegm and launched it at the stranger's back.

Cal felt the spray on his cheek. He had intended once again to deny the association, but that was the final straw; nobody had to stomach that kind of treatment. Yet still he tried to avoid a fight. Pushing himself off the bar, he turned to address the nervous

24

card players.

But the icy control that was an essential facet of life to a gunfighter began to crumble.

'Can't one of you guys handle this jumped up whippersnapper,' he railed. 'The snotty-nosed kid needs his ass paddling. And if none of you can do it then I will.'

But Billy Vance's sidekicks remained tight-lipped as they edged out of the line of fire.

Vance's tanned features assumed a purple hue. The young tough was incensed, beyond the point of no return. Cal Gentry had affronted his dignity and the offence demanded satisfaction. As far as Billy was concerned, there was only one way that could be achieved. The kid went for his gun.

His right hand only managed to fold around the bone handle of the much prized Colt revolver before he staggered back, surrounded by a haze of gun-smoke. Arms windmilling, he crashed into a table.

Nobody had seen Cal Gentry move. Yet his own pistol, smoke twining from the barrel, had seemingly leapt into his right hand. A single shot was all that was needed. Billy Vance would not be getting back to his feet.

As the discordant echo died away, Cal kept the gun trained on the inert form. Thumb curled round the hammer, he waited, just in case the kid was playing possum. It had happened before. Bill Hickok had told him always to go for a killing shot.

'Wound a man and he always retains the option of shooting back.'

That poignant assertion from the renowned gun-fighter had stuck with Cal and saved his bacon on more than one occasion.

Unfortunately it was a cowardly act that cut short Wild Bill's life. It happened back in 1876 while he was playing cards in a Deadwood saloon. Jack McCall was a bad loser. Even after the celebrated lawman offered to buy him breakfast, McCall snook up behind and gunned him down in the back that same night. But he paid for his rash action by being the principle guest at his own necktie party.

'You saw it, didn't you?' Cal asked the barman.

'Sure did, Mister Gentry sir. He drew first.'

'And you fellas?'

They all nodded.

'Don't matter none though,' observed the medita-tive doctor. 'Billy has two brothers. And they ain't gonna bother a hoot who drew first. You'd be well advised to get outa town fast.'

It was sound advice.

Cal kept his gun on the gaping occupants of the saloon as he backed out of the door.

'Don't nobody move until I'm clear of town,' he ordered. 'And be sure to tell the law who started this. I don't need any more dodgers claiming that Cal Gentry is a murdering skunk.'

'Good luck, mister,' murmured the medic, more to himself than the fleeing gunfighter. 'I figure you're going to need it. Eugene and Nathan Vance ain't about to let this drop.'

The others nodded in sympathy.

'He may be lightning fast on the draw but those guys play dirty,' muttered Chuck Raisin sucking on a dead cigar.

THREE

CORONADO MESA

Cal spurred away from Tucumcari at a fast lick heading south west across the bleak sagebrush wilderness. Two hours passed before he paused on a low rise to survey his backtrail. No tell-tale signs of rising dust. His fervent hope was that his pursuers had been thrown off the scent once he left the main trail. Rider and horse slowed to an easy canter.

Darkness had enfolded the featureless terrain when Cal finally made camp for the night on the banks of a broad expanse of water known as The Blue Hole. Much as he would have welcomed a pot of coffee and some hot food, discretion won the battle.

It would be a cold supper of hardtack biscuits and beef jerky washed down by cold water. By spreading a slicker over his head, Cal did manage a couple of smokes before settling down for the night under a blanket of twinkling stars.

But sleep eluded the gunfighter. This darned reputation was following him around the country like a bad smell. All he could hope was that the further west he travelled, the less likelihood there was that any nosey bartenders would eyeball him.

'Anything out there, Eugene?' inquired a yawning Nathan Vance while scratching at his bulging gut. The bleary-eyed roughneck sat up then ran a hand through a mop of greasy black hair. Nathan had always been the laziest of the clan but that didn't make him any less eager to avenge his kid brother's shooting. Family loyalty demanded an eye for an eye, and maybe an arm and a leg as well.

His brother had been assiduously studying the bleak terrain of early morning since sunup. No way was he about to let this critter escape through their clutches. Eugene's face was set in a granite hard scowl – Cal Gentry had met his match by gunning down one of the Vance Brothers.

'Not yet!' came back the curt response. 'Now get yourself out of that pit and set the coffee brewing. I've been up two hours already.'

Nathan grunted before setting the blackened pot to boil.

That was a big mistake.

Cal had also been up and on the trail before dawn. He had been following a narrow deer run that meandered between desiccated clumps of mesquite and greasewood. The drabness of the grim wasteland was relieved only by occasional stands of Yucca. The creamy white blossoms were sometimes known as *Our Lord's Candlesticks.*

The sun was lifting gracefully into an azure firmament when his pace slowed on the approach to a surging wall of red sandstone. From afar, Coronado Mesa appeared to be an impregnable obstacle. Closing the distance, though, a clear gap soon emerged. Gallino Pass afforded the only means of penetrating the rocky barrier, a narrow trail no more than a horse width snaked up a tortuous and stony route from the desert floor.

Cal slowed to a walk, eyes on the alert for an ambush. If the Vance Brothers had got here ahead of him, this would be the ideal spot to launch an attack. A loose smile broke across his austere expression. It seemed like the Good Shepherd was keeping a watchful eye on this member of his flock.

His eagle vision had picked up a rising plume of white smoke. Thin as a rope, it filtered up from behind a cluster of boulders in the notched gap marking the entrance to the Pass. Cal drew to a halt and dismounted. Ground hitching the paint behind a large rock, he carefully studied the telltale giveaway. His weathered features evoked a bleak frown.

Knowing the territory, these guys had figured out his likely route and gotten here in advance. But a brazen presumption that their quarry was a naïve tenderfoot had made them careless. Cal checked his six-gun then picked a circumspect path up the rough gradient. His intention was to circle round and come at the bushwackers from above and behind.

'He oughta be here by now,' snapped a waspish Eugene Vance sipping at his coffee.

'You reckon he's come this way?' asked Nathan chewing on a strip of burnt fatback. 'Maybe he took the southern trail by way of Fort Sumner.'

The suggestion received a snort of disdain.

'No chance! Guys like Gentry avoid the military.' Eugene's bullet head bobbed. 'And this is the only place through the Coronados.'

'You're sure right there, fellas,' breezed a perky voice from behind. 'A pity for you that fat boy here couldn't rein up his need for hot grub.'

Both of the men stiffened. Cal's sudden appearance had momentarily stunned the pair of ambushers. Slowly they turned to face the object of their hatred. He was stood atop a rocky shelf overlooking their camp.

Eugene was the first to recover. His mouth bent down in an ugly snarl.

'Don't try it, mister!' rasped Cal discarding his previous easy manner as Eugene's left hand dropped to his holstered revolver. 'There's a lead messenger here just itching to make your acquaintance.'

The elder brother slowly raised his hands, his sharp eyes never leaving the gunfighter. But Nathan was not so easily cowed. He was equally as hotheaded as his younger brother and always apt to exhibit less caution than Eugene. But worst of all, he hated being referred to as *fat boy*. Without any thought for the consequences, he grabbed the Henry carbine lying

31

beside his bedroll, jacked a round up the spout, and spun.

Two shots rang out. The sharp cracks rebounded off the confining walls of the Pass. Both took Nathan Vance in the chest punching him back across the burning embers of the campfire. His clothes quickly caught alight; the cloying stench of burning flesh permeated the air of the killing ground.

Cal ignored the grim scenario as he carefully approached the camp.

'Now take off your boots,' he ordered the remaining Vance brother. Eugene offered him a dumb look of bewilderment. 'You heard, knucklehead,' repeated the testy gunfighter. 'I said off with them goddamed boots! And be quick about it. That half-wit brother of your'n is getting a mite overdone.'

To lend emphasis to the command, Cal loosed a couple of slugs at the bushwacker's feet. That spurred him into action. The shots, assisted by a sharp slap on their rumps from Cal, propelled the two horses down the trail.

'Being cow ponies, they'll find their own way back to the home base,' he said, 'Now it's time you was joining them. On your way!'

'You can't leave me out in this godforsaken wilderness without boots or a mount.' The statement from Eugene Vance was less a plea for clemency, more the startled realization that he was the victim of his own brash presumption.

'I can, and just did.' Extracting a large Bowie knife from a sheath on his left side, Cal slashed the scuffed boots to ribbons which he threw down at the other's bare feet. 'So you'd be advised to get moving now, mister,' snapped the gunfighter, 'else it won't only be your brother who'll be providing a cooked breakfast for them there buzzards.'

His head shifted to a row of three birds perched on a dead tree branch. Discordant squawks of agreement accompanied this suggestion.

'At least give me a canteen of water,' pleaded the bootless felon.

After helping himself to a mug of coffee, Cal toed the smouldering body of Nathan Vance aside.

'At least you make a decent brew,' remarked the gunfighter picking up one of the canteens and tossing it across to the hovering villain. 'Now shift your ass.' Another shot kicked up sand at the critter's feet encouraging him to get started on the long and painful journey home. A mocking shout of derision pursued the departing footslogger. 'And be sure not to step on any rattlers.'

Cal waited until the guy was well down the trail and out of sight before he sat down and took advantage of the food left by the skulking pair of backshooters. It was another half hour before he mounted up to continue his journey in the opposite direction.

What he had failed to heed, however, was that Eugene Vance was not so easily swayed from his mission of vengeance. Scrambling up to the top of a ridge overlooking Gallino Pass, he raised a hand to shield out the sun's glare. A mirthless smile cracked the hard demeanour.

Vance was well satisfied with his tough climb. It had paid dividends. Gentry was heading south west. And the only town in that direction was Socorro. It was five days by horse, but Eugene wasn't worried.

He had a cousin who ran a horse ranch north of the Guadalupe Range at Santa Rosa. It was no more than five hours' walk from the Pass although without boots it might well take him the rest of the day. Grit and an iron determination to avenge not one but two brothers would ensure that he made it.

'You better watch your back, Mister Lightning Gunfighter,' muttered the burly dirt farmer under his breath. 'Eugene Vance ain't about to give up until you're the one that's buzzard bait.' A manic chortle issued from between clenched teeth. 'Then we'll see who's kissing the sidewinder.'

FOUR

CURSED BY FATE

The gunfighter had much to think on during the next phase of his journey.

Five years had passed since he last set eyes on his wife and son. The boy would now be seven. A lump formed in Cal's throat. It was always the same when morose thoughts concerning his estranged family surfaced.

Grit-scoured eyes peered into the distance as he left the soaring wall of the Coronado Mesa behind. Ahead lay an arid landscape covered with scrub vegetation dominated by saltbush and blue gramma where herds of buffalo wandered. Intermittent banks of low hills flanked by clusters of juniper and ponderosa pine relieved the dull monotony.

The steady jogging of the paint enabled his meditations to once again drift back to a more idyllic period when life promised far more than it ultimately delivered. He was back in Salina, Kansas having stopped off to replenish his supplies en route to the exciting prospects offered by Dodge City.

The trail-weary rider drew his mount to a halt outside a store that advertised '*Everything you ever wanted – and more!*'. He slapped the dust from his torn and grubby duds. It sounded just the kind of emporium he was after. A jingling bell announced his presence. The store was clearly open, yet empty. No customers, not even a counter clerk.

'Anyone at home,' hollered the newcomer.

A tiny voice cut through the silence.

'Be with you in a minute!'

It appeared to be coming from a back room.

Suddenly the pleasantly lyrical cadence degenerated into a frightened cry that was followed immediately by a discordant pandemonium. Something was clearly amiss. Without preamble, Cal Gentry vaulted over the counter and ran into the back room.

There he came across a young woman sitting on the floor amidst a clutter of tin plates and buckets. She seemed to be physically unhurt. Only her pride had suffered as she took heed of the stranger blocking the doorway. Cal couldn't resist a wry smile.

'Don't just stand there gawping,' squealed the blushing girl trying to hide her chagrin at being discovered in this unflattering position. 'Help me up.'

'S-sure thing, miss,' stammered the goggle-eyed customer hurrying forward.

Once returned to a comportment more becoming

36

to a young woman, she raised a haughty eye to the young stranger and continued with her duties as if nothing untoward had so recently occurred.

'Can I help you, sir?' she warbled in a lofty tone that attemped to regain her injured poise.

Cal easily saw through the subterfuge, but quickly swallowed the chuckle gurgling in his throat to save the girl further discomfort. After all, even with the dusty mark on her pert nose and auburn hair bent askew, she was decidely pleasing on the eye.

'I need some new duds,' he said struggling to maintain a rather strained deadpan look. 'A couple of shirts, jacket and a pair of corduroys.'

The clerk nodded her agreement with an imperious sniff as she ran a disparaging eye over the trail-worn customer. A languid arm indicated the location of the required items. 'You will find we have a wide choice of clothing suitable for all occasions, and *people*.' Emphasis on this last word was meant to restore her confidence.

Cal acknowledged the attempted rebuke with a spirited bow.

After selecting and paying for his purchases, he made to leave the store.

'I'll be staying in town for a few days on business,' he said while opening the door. 'Perhaps we might . . . bump into each other again.' A sly grin spread across the rugged countenance.

The girl's smoothly aquiline cheeks reddened, but she couldn't help returning the smile. This enigmatic stranger might be a touch forward, but he certainly had entrancing grey eyes that held her in their mesmeric embrace. It was an alien feeling that was both exciting yet confusing.

Miss Cecelia Featherstone felt a little giddy and had to clutch hold of the counter to steady herself.

'Perhaps,' she murmured abstractedly as the door closed.

Cal had likewise been affected in a way that was alien to his usual encounter with the fairer sex. Most of his previous run-ins were with less scrupulous dames who demanded hard cash up front. The frank honesty of the girl's naive innocence had touched him to his very core.

Four days passed before the unlikely duo met up again. On this occasion, it was under less agreeable circumstances.

Cal had been investigating the possibility of sinking his funds into a cattle buying enterprise. The herds coming north up the trail from Texas had led to a boom period in the business of beef export to the big cities of Chicago and the East. There were a number of options under consideration but thus far, nothing had been agreed. Maybe he would have better luck in Dodge.

It was early evening and the saloons were just beginning to fill up. Strolling along the boardwalk, Cal's thought were fixed on to the various deals he had been investigating.

Raucous laughter up ahead outside one the numerous drinking dens along Glendale Street jerked him out of his reflective musings. A bunch of cowpokes, clearly the worse for wear, had hustled out on to the boardwalk and were blocking the way. Cal surmised that they had only recently been paid off and were hellbent on making up for lost drinking time.

Nothing wrong with that. Just so long as they didn't bother anyone.

But it was not to be.

A frightened howl of indignation issued from somewhere within the swaying mêlée. It sounded like a woman's cry for help. In most frontier settlements, ladies were accorded due respect by the predominantly male population. But drink was always likely to blur a man's natural regard for this accepted law of the frontier.

And this appeared to be just such a case in point.

Cal noticed a blue dress attempting to push aside the pawing hands. He hurried onward intent on remedying what was rapidly degenerating into an ugly scene. On drawing close he saw that it was the store clerk from whom he had purchased his current apparel. A cold frown puckered his brow.

Without preamble he drew his pistol and slammed the barrel down on the nearest head. The owner grunted and went down in a heap. With his free hand, Cal aimed a brutal punch to the stubbly jaw of a heavy set jasper who was attempting to kiss the terrified girl. The guy's head snapped back. A second equally devastating blow sent the cowboy's eyes spinning as he joined his buddy on the floor.

The gun panned across the remaining drunks.

Mouths agape, they tottered back out of reach of the lethal assailant, bleary heads rapidly throwing off the alcoholic fuzz.

'Anyone else want trouble?' snarled Cal skewering the three remaining cowboys with a regard that promised dire consequences should the wrong answer be forthcoming. At the same time, he drew the girl to one side away from the recent danger. 'Cos I'm more than ready to accommodate.'

'The boys didn't mean nothing, mister,' interjected a grizzled older guy who had just emerged from the saloon. Bracken Spriggs was their ramrod and trouble was the last thing he needed. 'Just a little funnin', that's all. There's no harm done.'

'I don't call it fun hassling a young lady going about her lawful business,' replied the irate gunfighter steadying his revolver. 'Now if you fellas apologize like I know you're going to, we'll say no more about it.'

Nobody moved.

The ramrod offered the tall stranger a closer look. His eyes widened. He'd set eyes on this dude before in Abilene. Unless he defused the tense stand-off, blood would surely be spilled.

'You heard the man, knuckleheads!' he yelled anxious to get his hands away. 'Say you're sorry and let's skidaddle. And next time, you'd best not rile this guy.'

'Why not?' came the belligerent response from one young firebrand.

'Ever heard of Lightning Cal Gentry?'

The name drew gasps from the hovering cowboys who peered sheepishly at each other. The gunfighter's name had become legendary in the last few years. A series of muted apologies quickly issued from the subdued cowhands who now realized the error of their ways as they backed off. Spriggs promised himself that back at camp, some of these reckless saddle bums would get more than a tongue-lashing.

Cal nodded his acceptance that the altercation was over as he placed a protective hand around the girl's waist and led her across the street to the Palace Diner.

'Perhaps you would allow me to buy you a strong cup of coffee?' he suggested to the bemused young lady. 'And perhaps a meal to follow?'

Miss Featherstone broached no objections to the intimate though no less welcome support, allowing herself to be taken in hand. The repellent incident had shaken her up.

'Didn't I say that we would meet up again soon?' smiled the handsome paladin. 'Although I would have preferred it to be under more pleasant circumstances.'

The cowboys from the Wagon Wheel trail drive had followed their boss up the street, his blistering comments ringing in their ears.

Only one remained behind. Wes Chainey stumbled to his feet and rubbed his sore head, shaking the cloud of mist away. An ugly sneer hissed from between pursed lips. Nobody slugged Chainey without payment and the wild kid knew exactly what kind of redress he wanted.

He had ignored the ramrod's curt order. Now he stood poised in the middle of the street, legs spaced apart, body hunched over as he flexed his gunhand. Hate-filled black eyes bored menacingly into the gunfighter's back.

'Hold it right there, Gentry!'

The brusque summons, clear and unequivocal, drilled into Cal's brain. He knew that call. He had heard its like on many previous occasions. He halted abruptly. Extricating Cecelia's welcome hands from his own, he quietly and calmly told her to wait for him in the diner.

Then he swung on his heel. A fluid decisive movement found him facing the snarling face of his adversary. Once again this would be a duel to the finish, no quarter asked nor given. Only one man would remaining standing.

All the same, he tried.

'You can walk away now, mister,' he called to the rigid figure of Wes Chainey. 'No loss of face. Better a live cowpoke than a dead gunslinger.'

But there was no going back for the young gunnie who saw fame and fortune staring him in the face, rather than a boot hill tombstone.

The man who shot down Cal Gentry. It sounded good. A heap better than punching cows. Impatiently he waved away the gesture.

'You scared then, mister?' he rasped.

Cal ignored the jibe.

'Just make your play!' he hissed adopting his own stance.

Seconds passed. Glendale Street had emptied. Bullets were about to fly and nobody wanted to be in the firing line, although a myriad eyes peered out from the safety of adjacent buildings.

Then it happened: Chainey slapped leather. It was the slight lifting of the right shoulder that was the telltale sign.

Cal's gun barrel was smoking. A hole in the centre of the pretender's chest oozed blood as he wobbled unsteadily. Two bullets ploughed into the dirt at the cowboy's feet as finger muscles contracted in death. Then, in slow motion, he slumped forward on to his face.

The gunfighter remained still, unmoving. It was the town lawdog's gruff voice that broke into thoughts that enshrined no elation, no surge of excitement. Only sorrow that yet another life had been wasted unnecessarily.

'OK, mister,' declared the marshal with a heavy sigh. 'You can leather that hogleg now.' Tom Patton was no tenderfoot law officer, he had come across all manner of gunslingers. No matter how innocent they claimed to be, all attracted grief and tribulation like bees to a jampot. 'I saw it all. He called you out and drew first. But I want you out of this town today. A gunfighter like you is trouble which we don't need in Salina.'

Cal merely nodded. He knew the score.

'Just give me time to say my goodbyes.' The

request held a crushed, defeated feel. 'Then I'll be on my way.'

The lawman responded with a brusque nod.

'A half hour and no more.'

Cecelia Featherstone was likewise overcome, stunned by the sudden and violent revelations that had invaded her mundane existance. One minute she was walking down the street, the next hassled by drunken cowboys. Then saved by a knight in shining armour who turns out to be nothing more than a killing machine.

Much as he tried to justify himself, Cal failed miserably. Cecelia Featherstone, who had become the girl of his dreams was now merely an illusory fantasy, a figment of his fevered imagination. He had intended on just passing through Salina. This girl had persuaded him to stay. Now once again, his past had intervened.

Where would it all end?

He flicked away a teardrop threatening to undermine the tough persona. Then, with shoulders hunched, he nudged the paint down Salina's main drag, leaving behind much more than yet another town where he was not welcome.

FIVE

UNEXPECTED REUNION

A journey that ought to have lasted no more than five days took seven. This was due to a sandstorm which blew up while he was crossing a desolate stretch of white sand known as The Malpais. Undulating dunes akin to the ocean's swell rolled away to the distant horizon, finally crashing against the noble upsurge of the Sierra Oscura mountain range.

With no shelter to temper its might, the turbulent winds frequently swept up the dry sand into a fermenting maelstrom whose fury knew no bounds. Some storms blew themselves out in a matter of hours, others lasted for days. A week of unremitting blizzard conditions was not unusual. In these circumstances, the unlucky traveller had no option but to bed down behind whatever cover was available and weather it out.

Such was the fate of Cal Gentry.

He knew the sandstorm was coming an hour before it struck suddenly and without mercy. Visibility was reduced to zero as the howling blast enveloped horse and rider in a stinging embrace. Any skin exposed to the fierce scouring would have been scrubbed raw.

Huddling beneath a yellow rain slicker, Cal was forced to sit tight behind the welcome body of his mount. He was lucky. On the second day, the incessant scream of the wind gradually abated as the sandstorm passed on its way.

Within half an hour, a strangely silent calm had settled over the blanched wilderness. Blue sky dusted by a few cotton wool clouds gave no hint of the seething ferment that had so recently striven to hammer the gunfighter's huddled form into submission.

Peering out from his refuge, Cal heaved aside the thick layer of wind-blown sand. It was a further hour before horse and rider were rid of the gritty invasion to their personages; the white aggressor had gotten into everything.

It was another two days before the ancient adobe walls of Socorro hove into view. Cal heaved a gentle sigh of relief that his navigation had been sound. During its chequered history, the town had given shelter to the Hopi, Apache and Commanche tribes.

But it was the Spanish explorers who had transformed Socorro into the thriving place it had become by the year 1881. A centre for the cattle and sheep outfits within the locality, Socorro as its named suggests, offered succor and relief to trail-worn drifters, an oasis amidst the seering heat of the implacable desert.

But the town's real importance stemmed from it being the last stopping off point before traders tackled the dreaded *Jornada del Muerto*. Translated this means 'Journey of Death', and it was well named. Cal had just sampled and survived its unforgiving nature. Spanish traders were forced to brave the protracted, waterless desert on a regular basis in order to reach the Mexican border town of El Paso.

Since leaving Coronado Mesa, the gunfighter had not set eyes on a single human being. Now he ogled the teams of ox-drawn wagons laden with all manner of goods which filled the wide main street. Indians had disappeared from the sidewalks, replaced by ornately sombreroed Spanish grandees. American Stetsons were also prominently displayed.

In addition to the prevailing adobe structures, brick and wood were also becoming standard building materials. It was opposite one of the latter that Cal Gentry drew his jaded mount to a halt. The sweating paint took full advantage of the pause to slake her thirst at an adjacent water trough. Cal's gaze was drawn to a small store on the opposite side of the dusty street.

A lump stuck in his throat as he absorbed the name painted above the window.

Cecelia Featherstone – Dressmaker.

So she had reverted to her maiden name. Cal

shrugged. Could he blame her? What woman would choose to be associated with an infamous gunslinger? All the same, it stuck in his craw.

For fifteen minutes, he sat astride the patient horse, just staring at the shop, trying to probe the dim interior for some sign of movement. She was clearly inside – two customers had entered and left with packages under their arms.

He had finally girded his loins to make a move when suddenly, out of nowhere, a young kid dashed into the street chasing a ball from an adjoining alley. His whole attention was fixed on retrieving the bouncing object. Like any main street, that in Socorro was a bustling thoroughfare.

At that moment, a group of recently paid-off cowboys came charging down the street at a fast gallop. Heehawing and hallooing, a race was clearly in progress. Without thinking, Cal leapt from the saddle and scooped the boy up into his arms. Diving to one side, he felt a sharp stab of pain in his right shoulder as a pounding hoof connected. The excited riders thundered past in a cloud of billowing dust, completely unaware of the danger they had unwittingly precipitated.

'You all right, kid?' asked his concerned saviour glaring at the backs of the disappearing riders. He helped the startled youth to his feet. Both were covered in dust.

'Guess so,' stuttered the gaping boy unsure as to what had occurred.

'Next time you cross a street,' admonished the tall

stranger once he knew the kid was unharmed, 'make sure to look both ways, cos there might not be a helping hand to save your bacon. Savvy?'

A stern eye pierced the tremulous frame.

The object that had precipitated the boy's rash action lay in the middle of the street. It had been stamped into a mis-shapen lump of leather. Cal extracted a dime from his pocket and flipped it into the air.

'Here!' He smiled. 'Buy yourself a new one.'

The boy deftly caught the spiralling coin.

'Gee thanks, mister,' he gushed.

'Now run along,' said Cal ruffling the kid's tousselled locks. 'And mind how you go.'

After returning the smile, the kid then proceeded to ignore the stranger's sound advice by dashing into the street. Cal shook his head. They never learned. But it was the boy's destination that stiffened the man's square jaw, educing a tight-lipped gaze.

He had headed directly for the dressmaker's shop and disappeared inside.

Cal sucked in a deep breath and held it.

Could it be? It was five years since he had been forced to leave the family home in Nebraska; kids can change an awful lot in that time. And now here he was, gaping open-mouthed across the street like a love-sick yearling.

Then he saw her. A pale face peering warily through the window. Her stark beauty, etched against the dark interior of the shop, brought a cutting ache to his pounding heart. The image quickly disappeared, no doubt equally startled, though perhaps in a less endearing fashion.

Following Cal's ignominious exit from Salina, the two had met again by chance in Dodge City back in '73. Their courtship had been brief but impassioned. A quiet marriage had quickly followed after which they had left to start up a new life in the small town of Brady, Nebraska.

All seemed to be going well until Cal's notorious past caught up with them. It was the same old story: a Wanted dodger, a bounty hunter, and another killing. Once again, he was forced to go on the run from the pursuing lawmen. This time he was determined to start again in a far flung outpost where the name of Lightning Cal Gentry meant nothing, where the spurious reputation as an outlaw and killer had failed to penetrate.

Was there such a place?

The girl, now mother to his son, decided there was not. The distraught farewell that neither wanted had become inevitable. Many words, arguments, entreaties had passed back and forth before the woeful parting of the ways.

The gunfighter's only solace was that he had managed to extract a promise that someday they would be reconciled. It was granted, but only when he could guarantee the safety of his family through total anonymity. Being recognized in Tucumcari had been a severe blow to the fulfillment of his ambition.

Cal figured that moment had arrived when he left Kansas. Returning to Brady in Nebraska, he had learned that Cecelia had left the town over a year before. Nobody had any idea of her destination. Only in the last few months had he learned from a passing muleskinner that a certain dressmaker by the name of Featherstone had set up in the New Mexico town of Socorro.

'Didn't expect to see you around these parts, Cal.'

The gruff announcement jolted the nervous watcher from his reverie. Stung into action, he immediately reverted to gunfighter mode. His hand dropped to the holstered six shooter as he spun to face this unexpected threat. The first thing he saw was the glinting tin star pinned to a broad chest.

'I don't know whether I ought to pleased to see you, or worried sick,' continued the wary speaker.

That was the moment Cal recognized his old side-kick.

His mouth dropped open.

'Don't worry,' grinned the marshal holding up a placatory hand. Then lowering his voice, he added, 'I ain't about to arrest the notorious Lightning Cal Gentry.'

Cal finally found his voice.

'Kansas Jack Tillman!'

The name was uttered in a tone that evoked a mixture of surprise and suspicion, but was also laced with a measure of respect and admiration. The pair had been close buddies at one time.

'What in tarnation are you doing here?' asked the startled newcomer. 'Last I heard you were up north in the Dakotas trying your hand at prospecting.'

'That game's for the birds,' snorted the lawman.

'And what's with the badge?' Cal jabbed a finger at the shiny tin star.

Kansas Jack smiled.

'When the gang broke up, me and some of the boys headed up that way, but we couldn't shake off the law. The others were killed in an ambush. I managed to escape and figured the only sensible option was if'n you can't beat 'em, then join 'em.' A terse grunt followed. 'Seemed like a safer bet all round. So I came down here where nobody knew me. And it's worked out good. Socorro's a nice town.'

Tillman arrowed a bleak look towards his one-time buddy. 'And that's how I wanna keep it. You get my drift, Cal?'

'You want me out of your town. That the notion, Jack?'

'You got it in one, buddy.'

'And that's just what I intend to do,' Cal intoned firmly. 'All I want is to persuade Cecelia and the boy to go with me to Arizona. Nobody will know me out there. And we can start again from scratch.'

'Don't reckon she'll want to see you, Cal.' The reformed outlaw's voice had hardened, his delivery candid and granite-edged. 'She's told the boy that his pa died of the fever,' continued the flat voice from behind a thick moustache. A dour regard held the gunfighter.

The two men faced each other. Jack Tillman knew that he was no match for his old partner in the leather-slapping stakes. But he was no weakling, and

52

held his ground. It was the gunfighter who backed off. He had no wish to precipitate trouble.

His bleak expression softened as he relaxed his stance. Removing his hat, Cal ran a hand through the thatch of sandy hair.

'All I wanna do is talk to her, Jack,' he pleaded. 'And see the boy. Least you can do is allow me that. If she don't listen, at least I've tried. Then I'll leave town. What d'yuh say, buddy?'

Kansas Jack huffed some. He had his own reasons for wanting Cal Gentry out of Socorro.

Cecelia Featherstone was a mighty handsome woman. And the marshal had been hoping to place their growing friendship on to a more intimate level. Cal Gentry's inauspicious arrival on the scene would place that in jeopardy. He could only hope that her assertion that he was out of her life for good would hold true.

'I'll try to set up a meeting,' Tillman conceded trying to hide his concern. 'But it's up to her. If she refuses, I don't want you getting sassy.'

Cal noted the tough line that his old buddy was adopting, but responded with a curt nod of the head. 'If that happens, I'll leave town and you'll never see me again.'

That appeared to satisfy the lawman.

'Wait in the saloon,' he replied. 'I'll send you word of her decision.'

With that, the two sidekicks parted. Tillman headed back to his office to consider how best to play this unexpected occurrence. Cal Gentry needed that drink to calm his jangling nerves, to consider his options should Cecelia refuse to see him.

It was an hour before Tillman returned.

'Any luck?' inquired an unusually skittish Cal Gentry.

He felt more nervous than on his wedding day. Would she agree to see him? The question kept shifting round inside his head until he had convinced himself that the answer would be a resounding '*No*'.

The marshal ordered a stiff whiskey and slung it down before answering. He sucked in a deep breath, pushing his hat back.

'She's prepared to give you ten minutes and no more. And the boy mustn't know that you're his father.'

Cal emitted a huge sigh of relief.

'But what about us going to Arizona?' he blurted out.

Tillman shrugged.

'You'll have to discuss that with her yourself,' he said. 'But I wouldn't be getting your hopes up. She seemed pretty much aggrieved that you'd turned up out of the blue just when she was hoping to put the past well and truly behind her.'

Cal poured another snort and sunk it in a single draught. The hard liquor burned a path down his throat. Levering his taut frame off the bar, he gave his old buddy a curt nod of appreciation then headed for the street. There he hovered, uncertainty clouding his thoughts. Finally he crossed to the far side. Another hesitant pause followed as his sticky hand rested on the door handle of the the dressmakers' emporium.

For half a minute his body refused to move, tense nerves had clamped him up tighter than a whore's corset. It was a muted yet familiar voice from inside that released the locked muscles.

'If'n you've got some'n to say, then come in and get it off your chest.' Same old Cecelia. Just like he remembered her. Direct, straight to the point, no flannelling with the issue.

She was busy sewing up a piece of fabric when he entered the store. No greeting, no smile of welcome. And no further remarks uttered. The girl's eyes remained lowered. Intent on continuing the job in hand, she refused to meet his fervent gaze. Only when Cal deigned to voice a greeting of his own did she finally look up.

'Good to see you, Cec,' he mouthed barely above a hoarse whisper. 'It's been a long time.'

'Not long enough far as I'm concerned,' she said, brazenly trying to maintain an aloof bearing. Then with a feisty rebuttal snapped, 'And don't be calling me Cec. You know how it rankles.'

Cal responded with a bashful look of apology.

His wife threw down the material she had been sewing then launched into a blistering verbal assault. 'Me and little Joe are trying to start a new life down here far away from the hell-raising and gunplay that always followed you around.'

That was the start of an impassioned harangue,

fiery and torrid. A fervent denouement that had been festering in her soul for five long years. Now, all the heartache, the grief and sorrow came gushing forth like a raging creek that had burst its banks.

Cal remained silent throughout the scathing tirade. Head bowed, he allowed this winsomely bewitching creature whom he loved more than life itself to berate him unmercifully. He deserved it. She came round the counter, her tiny fists pummelling his broad chest. But eventually, just like an over-stretched horse, she ran herself into the ground.

That was when Cal stepped forward and placed a finger over her trembling lips instantly stilling the vapid outburst. Tears formed behind the large green saucers peering up at him, an irresitible witchery that wrenched his being to its very core.

Both of them knew. It was all a sham. A blatant front that now collapsed in a flood of anguish. Visions of all they had once meant, still meant to each other, surged forward.

Their lips met. Locked in a gossamer cocoon of bliss where nothing else mattered, the estranged husband and wife clung desperately together. Time stood still on a cloud of euphoric rapture. It was a howling dog that brought them back down to terra firma.

Eventually, some degree of normality returned, if such existed.

Cal reminded her of his vow to bury the infamous reputation that had been a constant drain on their happiness.

As for upping sticks and heading for Arizona, the girl stressed that such a course needed serious consideration. They parted with the firm understanding that Cecelia would talk it over with her son, but there were no promises.

Cal left knowing that he had done everything that was humanly possible. Now all he could do was wait until the following day when her decision would be announced.

Deep furrows creased the gunfighter's brow as he made a beeline for the saloon and that half finished bottle of hooch.

From his vantage point by a window above the jailhouse, Kansas Jack Tillman appraised the pensive figure slowly crossing the street. He had no way of knowing in which direction the assignation had gone. Was that a look of dejection, or one of elation on the unwelcome gunman's weathered visage?

Jack Tillman knew which he would prefer.

SIX

FLY IN THE OINTMENT

The two riders cautiously brought their mounts to a halt. On the far side of the swirling waters of the Rio Grande was the town of Socorro. Shielding out the westering sun, wary eyes probed the adobe structures. Both men leaned forward, hands resting on saddle horns.

After being cast afoot, Eugene Vance had made good time. Far better than he had expected.

His sidekick operated a horse ranch near Santa Rosa which Eugene had finally reached after seven painful hours. After bandaging up his cousin's bleeding feet, they had set off on two of the swiftest mounts on the ranch. Rowdy Bob Connor had been more than eager to join his cousin after learning that the infamous gunslinger, Lightning Cal Gentry, had shot and killed one of his kinfolk.

Scowling at the clutter of buildings, Eugene could only hope that his hunch regarding the killer's destination was sound. And that he was still here.

'No point just hanging around like spare parts,' he rasped setting his hat straight. Gently rowelling the feisty arab thoroughbred, he led the way across the trestle bridge. Shod hoofs echoed on the wooden slats like pistol shots. The comparison sat well with the avenger.

'How we gonna know if this dude is still around?' enquired Rowdy Bob loosening his pistol in its holster.

'Easy!' shot back Eugene, his black stubbled cheeks breaking into an evil grimace. 'I'd recognize that paint of his any place. And if'n the blamed cayuse ain't on the main street, we ask at the livery.'

They walked the horses up the shallow grade to the edge of the town before dismounting and hitching the mounts behind a crumbling wall.

Both men checked their handguns.

'You got a plan, Eugene?' inquired his cousin peering up the near empty street. Mid afternoon was the hottest time of day when most sensible folks were indoors enjoying a siesta.

Eugene considered the question with a measured degree of calculation. No sense blundering in half-cocked; their success required devious thought and cunning. A tense expectancy had heightened his awareness of the task he had set himself. He flexed the muscles in his gunhand. This was the moment of no return. The notion of backing out had not been contemplated. Revenge for the death of his younger kin was solidly entrenched in his black heart.

'You take the far side of the street,' replied the edgy Vance. 'I'll take this side. But make sure you stay ten paces behind me.' He then went on to explain the vital role that Rowdy Bob was to play in this deadly game of cat and mouse.

The blazing sun hammered the street from a cloudless azure sky. A slumbering cur raised its weary head as the stalking gunman slid past. The silence was broken by the rusty squeal of a barber's sign gently swaying in the gentle hot breeze.

An idyllic moment that was about to be shattered.

Halfway down the street, Eugene stumbled to a halt. His black eyes squinted out the glare, focusing on the distinct striations of black, brown and white daubed across the familiar paint mare's coat. It was tied to a hitching rail outside a dressmaker's store.

A mirthless grin cracked the crusty visage, quickly fading to a grimly resolute mould. He signalled to his sidekick. Connor responded with a raised hand before slipping out of view behind a stack of barrels; he was fully cognisant of what had to be done.

Eugene scanned the street in both directions. Still empty. Perfect.

Then he stepped down off the boardwalk and positioned himself in the middle of the rutted thoroughfare.

Inside the store, Cal was waiting for his wife to divulge whether they had a future together. The girl had been sitting for hours in the back room sifting her thoughts and desperately trying to reconcile the conflicting emotions washing around in her head.

Once again Cal rang the store bell. He knew she was here, otherwise the shop door would have been locked.

Cautiously she appeared. An uncertain regard, sad and rather forlorn, caused his pulse to race. Was this to be a knockback? It sure looked that way. His shoulders slumped.

'I guess you've decided to turn me down,' he said flatly, his voice low and full of sorrow.

'I want us to be together,' asserted the girl wringing her hands. 'It's just that I don't want to disrupt little Joe's life here. He's made friends. We've both made friends and got ourselves settled.' She took a breath. An imploring look fastened on to this man whom she loved with all her soul. 'Why do we have to move all the way to Arizona? You aren't known in these parts. Cal Gentry could easily bury his past. Start afresh.'

'What about Jack Tillman?' countered the gun-fighter. 'He knows my past. And he laid it on the line that he don't want me around.'

'I can bring Jack around,' she said eagerly. 'He'll listen to me.'

A shadow passed over Cal's rugged features. He frowned expressively.

'You and he ain't—'

Cecelia cut him off with a curt rebuttal.

'No! We are not,' she affirmed with vigour. A

disdainful snort of censure was the dressmaker's response to that accusation. 'Jack and I are just good friends. Nothing more.'

Cal relaxed, although a new aspect to his old buddy's intentions was elbowing itself to the forefront of his thoughts. Cecelia might not regard Jack Tillman as a potential beau, but Cal was not so sure. Maybe the marshal of Socorro harboured his own agenda in that direction. It was yet a further reason for them leaving the town and setting up elsewhere – a place where he could most definitely guarantee seclusion and privacy.

But the gunfighter was accorded no further opportunity to argue his case.

Outside, a strident challenge, blunt and unequivocal, called him out.

'I know you're in there, Gentry,' hollered the brittle snap from the street. 'Come out and meet your Maker, you murdering sonofabitch.'

That voice struck a chord. He knew it from somewhere, and recently too. Then it struck home. Eugene Vance. The critter must have somehow recovered his mount and followed him to Socorro aiming to complete the unfinished business of avenging his brother's demise.

Stunned by this unexpected resurrection of her husband's perfidious reputation, Cecelia now proceeded to vent her anger.

'You couldn't just leave us to get on with our lives in peace, could you?' she lambasted him. 'Had to come here and spoil things. And so once again, death has come a-calling.' She began to cry, turning her back. Her voice fell to a low murmur – an apathetic acceptance of the inevitability of life with this man. 'Just go and do what you have to. Then leave us be.'

'If'n you don't come out in one minute,' threatened the irate challenger, 'Then I'm coming in with all guns blazing, yuh lily-livered rat.'

Cal knew he had no choice but to face the antagonist. He ought to have shot the guy at Gallino Pass then none of this would have happened. Wishful thinking. Too late for that now.

Giving the girl one last despairing look, he walked to the door and stepped out into the light of day.

Eugene Vance offered him the devil's smile of a greeting.

'You ought never to have tangled with the Vance clan, mister,' he snarled settling himself ready for action. 'This is where you surrender that blamed reputation to a more worthy holder. Now say your prayers!'

That was the signal for Rowdy Bob to haul off from behind his place of concealment. Vance was no slick-assed gunman, and knew it. In a straight gunfight, he would be cut down before he had the chance to slap leather. This was his way of stacking the odds in his favour.

But fate chose that moment to step in on the side of Lightning Cal Gentry. The deep roar of a shotgun tore apart the static air on Main Street. Bob Connor staggered against the stack of barrels and pitched forward, sending them tumbling off the sidewalk. The large hole in his chest had terminated his cousin's slippery advantage.

Vance was momentarily thrown off guard by this unexpected shift in fortunes. Witnessing a sure-fire ploy dissolving before his eyes was like a red rag to a bull. Objective assessment of the situation was tossed aside. Three of his kin taken out by this gun-slinging rannie was too much. And that demanded retribution.

He went for his gun.

Cal was equally startled by the sudden change. He threw a quick glance towards the twirl of gunsmoke snaking from the entrance to an alley on the far side of the street. The stony regard of Marshal Jack Tillman met his enquiring eye. The lawman stepped out into the open.

'Drop your piece and surrender!' he ordered.

But Vance either didn't hear, or chose to disregard the summons. His filled hand lifted. Two shots rang out. Both from the spitting .45 of Cal Gentry. Each found its mark.

For the first time, however, they were not killing shots.

Cal was tired of all the gunplay. And he was also thinking of Cecelia.

One bullet struck Vance in the left arm, the other sent his hat spinning.

'Give yourself a chance, fella,' he called. It was almost a plea. 'Drop the gun and let's call it quits.'

'Never! Never!' screamed the rabid gun-toter. He

stepped forward, the pistol pointing and firing. Hot lead spewed forth. But his aim was wild, thrown off by the festering delirium that was eating away at his maniacal brain.

Cal knew he had to act quickly before a stray shot took him down. The next bullet creased the advancing man's head. It was enough to stun him into unconsciousness. He fell to the ground, out cold but still alive.

Cal's hands fell to his side, coils of white smoke twining from the hot barrel of his six-gun.

Faces started to appear at windows. Doors opened as onlookers emerged now the duel was over.

'Somebody get the doc,' shouted Tillman walking over to his old saddle partner.

'Much obliged, Jack,' said the gunfighter holstering his gun. 'You sure saved my bacon there and no mistake.'

'I was hoping to arrest the guy without any more gunplay,' replied the marshal lifting his shoulders in a weary shrug. 'But the darned fool had lost his marbles.' He raised a quizzical eyebrow. 'Word is that Cal Gentry always goes for the terminal shot. What happened here?'

'I'm through with all that.' Cal sighed. It was a mournful sigh like the last gasp of a dying rainstorm, or of a man hoping to bury his past, yet failing. 'There's been too much killing already. I'll be heading out in the morning,' he averred with a firm resolution. 'You were right, Jack. There's no place for me here.' Head lowered, he mumbled an abject finale. 'And I'll be going alone.'

The marshal stifled a smile of satisfaction.

But it was short lived.

'Not if I have anything to say in the matter.'

Both men turned as one to face this unexpected announcement.

'You mean. . . .' Cal was lost for words.

'Think I'd let you slip through my fingers again?' A beatific smile illuminated her radiant features. 'And that promise, about burying your past? I realize now that you meant every word. Letting that man live proved you want to start afresh. And I want to be a part of that.'

'What about the boy?' asked a wistful Cal Gentry. 'Does he cotton to some stranger lurching into his life, then persuading his ma to head out west and start again in some remote burg he's never heard of?'

'Joey's a good kid. He looks on it as a big adventure and can't wait to get started.'

That was all Cal wanted to hear.

For the first time in a coon's age, his seamed face split into a broad grin that registered pure elation. All the tension, the strain accumulated over years of dodging bullets and the law appeared to be over. He felt happier than he could ever have imagined possible. A new start beckoned with his family. What could be better?

But it was not what Kansas Jack had been expecting. Cecelia's sudden change of heart had come as a shock, and not one that he welcomed. Nonetheless, he smothered his true feelings and wished them well.

It was, in fact, upwards of a week before a fully laiden wagon was ready to leave town. Cecelia had arranged for one of her new customers to run the store during her absence with the option to purchase some time in the future.

In the meantime, Cal had talked the matter over with the marshal who had agreed to let the injured Eugene Vance off with a couple of weeks in jail and a fine once he had recovered from the gunshot wounds. A cunning hint that the hated gunfighter was southbound for Mexico would effectively steer the varmint on to a false trail.

SEVEN

YELLOW PERIL

The large iron key grated in the lock of the cell door.

'Time for you to leave, mister,' declared Marshal Tillman, adding with a twisted grin. 'Providing, of course, you can pay the fine.'

Vance growled as he sat up and scratched his ample belly – the flea-bitten mattress was making him itch. The grub wasn't upto much either. Although being allowed to leave following the disastrous shoot-out was something he sure hadn't expected.

He slanted a dubious half-open peeper at the hovering lawdog. What was this guy's angle? Disturbing the piece and threatening to kill someone merited six months' hard labour at the very least. Vance shrugged. Maybe getting shot up and made to feel like a greenhorn was punishment enough in this varmint's eyes.

'How much?' queried the prisoner.

Tillman leaned against the bars, a wicked looking knife deftly cleaning his finger nails. The ragged grimace did not give the impression that he was going to allow Vance just to walk out of the jail for a mere fine.

'Who said anything about money?' Tillman was like a cat playing a deadly game with a cornered mouse.

'I allus figured that a fine meant handing over a wad of greenbacks.'

'Not necessarily,' hinted the marshal who was clearly enjoying hmself. 'What if I was to let you out in exchange for a favour. A job that I want doing. One that I guarantee you will enjoy. I'll even include a week's supplies. Can't be fairer than that.'

Vance shook his head, clearly baffled.

'Stop playing games, Marshal,' he snapped, 'and get to the point. What are you really after?'

'How would you like to get even with Mister Calvin Gentry,' hissed Tillman, snapping the switchblade shut. 'Blow his lights out for good this time, and with my blessing.'

The dirt farmer's rheumy eyes widened. He sat up, back straight as an arrow. This was a reverse of fortunes he wouldn't have figured out in a million years. Then the penny dropped. So that was Tillman's angle.

'You've gotten the hots for that dame Gentry's come for,' smirked Vance. 'That's it. Now tell me if I'm wrong,' challenged the simpering felon.

Tillman lunged forward and grabbed the leering

toad. Hauling him to his feet, a couple of back-handers quickly wiped the smile from the felon's pudgy kisser. Blood dribbled from a split lip.

'You keep a civil tongue in your head,' Tillman snarled jamming his twitchy nose up close to the reeking sod-buster. 'I can always wait for the circuit judge to arrive. And he won't be so accommodating.'

Vance's response was a brittle snort of derision – the sod-buster was a tough cookie. The snarling glower quickly returned. He had the whip hand, and knew it.

'Then you wouldn't get this job done, would you marshal?'

There was no answer to that. And Tillman knew it. He threw the ugly cuss aside. 'Just watch your mouth, is all,' he huffed trying to regain the initiative. 'Me and him go back aways. There's unfinished business that ain't no concern of your'n. So how about it? Do we have a deal?'

This time it was Vance's turn to play the thoughtful card.

'Guess we do at that,' he concurred holding out a hand. 'Shake on it.'

Tillman reluctantly accepted the concilatory gesture.

'When it's done, I want to be informed,' he stressed, attempting to crush the other's paw. 'You make sure to come back this way so's I know that critter has well and truly hit the high road.' The lawman fastened an icy glare on to the killer as he presented his ultimatum. 'Otherwise I'll dog your trail. And when I catch up, you can look forward to being given the grand finale offered by the Georgia Send-Off.'

Vance gave him a quizzical frown, maintaining a deadpan expression to conceal the pain in his mashed hand.

'Target practice while hanging by your thumbs,' grinned the lawman.

Tillman was anxious for the hired gun to be on the trail. The circuit judge was due to arrive in Socorro in a week and he had no wish to be saddled with this guy for that. No telling what might come out in a trial, including his own nefarious association with the legendary gunfighter.

However, it was vital that the doctor and other leading citizens of Socorro did not cotton on to his clandestine scheme. It was a stroke of luck that on this particular morning, the medic had left town early to deliver a newborn at one of the local ranches. Likewise, the mayor was attending a miners' delegation in Albuquerque.

All the same, he was anxious to ensure that no other prying snoopers tuned into the plan which was why he had given the jailhouse swamper the morning off. Those guys were like gophers – they never missed a trick.

Tillman gingerly opened the back door. After checking the alley to ensure it was clear, he ushered the hired gunman outside where his saddled cayuse was patiently nibbling on some corn hocks.

The lawman grabbed a hold of the bridle before

the guy could spur off.

Fixing Vance with a look meant to embody both menace and entreaty, he spread the icing on the cake. 'Get Gentry out of the picture and there'll be a hefty bonus in it for you.'

Vance responded with a gruff smirk.

'This gal sure has gotten into your craw, marshal.' He shook his head in mockery. 'Some suckers'll do anything for a pretty face. More fool them! That's what I say.'

Without any further preamble, he gave the horse a vicious jab with his spurs and pounded off down the alleyway, disappearing through a huddle of outbuildings in a flurry of dust. Tillman cursed. His lip twisted into a brooding cusp. Maybe the only bonus you'll be receiving fella, he mumbled to himself, is one made of lead.

Vance was in a jaunty mood as he swung the horse towards the western Datil Mountains. Things were shaping up fine; he had escaped a jail sentence and been hired to rub out a hated enemy. The paymaster had even promised him a bonus.

It was a stabbing jolt of pain in his arm that reminded the gunman of Cal Gentry's contribution. He grimaced. A lethal sidewinder of that ilk would necessitate a notably cautious approach if the critter was to be dumped permanently. No more foolhardy schemes that were doomed to failure.

The killing of his two brothers further exemplified the fact that this venture was not just a paid undertaking. It was personal. A low grumble of anger rattled in his throat as the gunman remembered that the marshal had sealed his own fate by gunning down his cousin. Once he had the bonus pocketed, Eugene Vance intended to deliver his own bounty.

He slapped the six-gun strapped to his hip.

'You're gonna be kept mighty busy, Mr Colt,' he muttered. The growled imprecation was accompanied by a sinister leer.

He slowed the horse to a steady walk rubbing the bandage swathing the dent in his skull that still gave him a headache. Dark clouds were massing over the serated peaks of the Dantils indicating the approach of rain. They complemented the sombre vein that had settled over the gunman now that he fully appreciated the true nature of his task.

Jack Tillman had informed him of the subterfuge that he and Gentry had cooked up; a wild goose chase to throw any pursuer off the scent. The gunfighter and his family were supposedly travelling across The Malpais towards El Paso where allegedly they intended setting up home over the border in Mexico. In truth, they had headed west towards Arizona.

It was a large sprawling territory. Vance needed to have a more specific destination otherwise he would be no better off. All the lawman knew was that his old partner had always expressed a hankering to raise prime beef cattle. It was a dream he had harboured since they had first met back in Abilene.

The only place to which Tillman could put a name

was Safford in Arizona's Gila Valley. He had once seen it circled in pencil in a brochure for land purchase that Cal had sent for. The gang boss had remained tight lipped when questioned.

And that's all he knew. At least it offered a starting point once the hired killer reached Arizona. Vance scowled at the threatening storm clouds looming closer.

Six days passed before he encountered another human being.

Vance calculated that he was around three hours' ride from the small settlement of Pie Town which was the focus of mining activity on the North Plains of central New Mexico. Nudging his mount down a draw, he came across a pair of hoary old sourdoughs panning for gold.

'Howdie there!' hailed the newcomer.

The shabby duo remained silent, unmoving, their bodies tense.

'Any luck?' he posed, affecting a casual mien.

Both prospectors merely shrugged noncommitally. They sported heavy grey beards stained a dirty ochre from the corncob pipes each clenched between yellowed teeth. Steely eyes peered suspiciously from beneath thick brows.

'Nothing to speak of,' grunted the larger of the two eyeing the rider with cautious reserve. It was always best to maintain a deadpan expression in any talk of gold strikes with strangers.

'We're figurin' to move further up the draw if'n things don't improve,' remarked his partner leaning on a shovel.

Clad in mud-smeared corduroys and ragged coats, it was almost impossible to judge their ages. Bent backs and a weathered exterior was the lot of such prospectors.

Behind them stood a rough single room cabin with a pair of grubby cots visible through the open door. An old Hawken long rifle leaned against the wall. To one side, a smoke-blackened pan bubbled merrily, precariously resting on the embers of a spluttering fire. The noxious odour emanating from the unsavoury concoction produced a wrinkled sniff from the newcomer's twitching snout.

The miners shuffled uneasily.

Vance's searching gaze quickly spotted the casual toeing of a canvas bag into the shadow of a rocker box.

He smiled to himself. These guys were having more success than they were prepared to admit. And the supplies packed by Marshal Tillman were virtually exhausted. Not to mention his own empty pockets. Getting away from Socorro and the law had driven all else from his mind, but seeing that poke had resurrected the Devil in his soul.

He stored the information away before voicing his main reason for stopping.

'You boys seen a wagon pass this way recently?' An innocuously raised eyebrow accompanied the inquiry. 'Say in the last three weeks maybe?'

'Plenty of wagons pass this way, Mister,' grunted the smaller guy.

'And the drivers don't ask so many durned questions,' rasped his partner.

'It's my brother and his family,' Vance contrived forcing his tone to remain easy, innocent of any villainous intent. 'They're headed for Arizona. And I promised to meet them in Quemado when my business in Socorro was finished.' Wide eyed, harmless and gullible, he sought help from the two miners.

The ruse worked.

Both miners relaxed their stance.

'Seems like I do recall a family, now you mention it,' said the older guy scratching his dirty mop of hair. 'The fella called hisself Will Bennett. Said he was after running a beef spread near Safford.'

Vance stiffened. He recalled the bartender in Tucumcari declaring that his brother's killer had tried to pass himself off with that name. And Tillman's figuring that Safford was his destination had been proved right as well.

'That's them!' he smiled. 'Much obliged, fellas.'

Abruptly and without any warning, he drew his pistol and shot the older miner. The guy keeled over in a heap of rags.

Caught wrong-footed, his partner could only stare, mouth hanging ajar in astonishment. His eyes bulged at the sudden change in fortunes.

'Now, I'll take that poke you was trying to hide,' Vance snarled, swinging the smoking hogleg to cover the gaping sourdough.

No tenderfoot, the miner quickly recovered. He knew exactly where his fate lay. Throwing his stocky frame to one side, he grabbed for the loaded rifle and swung it towards this lowlife threat to his livelihood.

The sudden move had startled Vance's mount. The horse snickered, rearing up on to its hind legs.

That gave the miner a heaven-sent chance to avenge his partner. The Hawken boomed, its blackpowder charge echoing along the narrow draw. The horse took the full force of the load in its neck. Blood spurted from the fatal wound and the animal crumpled to the ground like a discarded rag doll. Vance managed to avoid the dead weight threatening to crush him.

With only one shot, the long rifle was now useless. The miner uttered a manic howl of fear. Discarding the gun, he turned to make a madcap dash along the edge of the creek. Vance allowed him the fantasy that escape was on the cards, a cruel delusion signified by the truculent smirk on the killer's face.

In no hurry, he removed the Henry carbine from its scabbard, jacked a round up the spout and took aim. All it took was a single shot. The miner threw up his arms and sprawled into the bed of the creek. He didn't get up. Dismounting, Vance heaved aside the rocker and extracted the bag underneath. His probing fingers reached inside playing with the nobbly contents, one of which he extracted.

The dull yellow metal elicited a nod of satisfaction.

With the brief shootout terminated, Vance suddenly felt ravenous; even the odious fair of miners becomes appetizing to a hungry man.

He stepped across to the simmering black pan. Raising the lid, his stomach lurched at the thought of refried beans and fatback. Nonetheless, he wolfed down the lot before secreting the poke inside his coat.

His belly full, Vance now turned his attention to shaking the dust from the killing ground. Water drifting downstream past the miners' camp soon espoused the appearance of a charnel house. Stained red with blood, it was a further reminder that he needed to make tracks. And quickly. There could be other prospectors in the vicinity. They might even have heard the fracas and be after investigating.

The main problem was that he had been cast afoot. And his only means of transport was a flea-bitten burro used by the miners. He shrugged. Once he reached Quemado, the gold would buy him a decent new mount.

Before leaving the isolated gold camp, he assiduously searched the cabin. But there were no signs of a further hidden cache, nor was there anything else worth appropriating. At least they had enough jerked beef and hard tack biscuits to see him through the next stage of his journey.

Retracing his steps back up the draw, Vance elected to avoid Pie Town and the chance of being questioned about the killings.

With some misgivings, he kicked the skittish burro into motion. Having to depend on a critter renowned for its stubborn belligerence meant avoiding all human contact, not merely on account of its lack of speed. Eugene Vance had his pride. And being spotted atop the lurching back of such a jackass might well lead to confrontations he could well do without. Much better to head direct for Quemado by a more circuitous route.

EIGHT

STROKE OF LUCK

As its name implies, Quemado had risen from the ashes of a previous wooden settlement that had burnt to the ground. To avoid another ignominious fate, the current town was built entirely of adobe bricks. Only the roofs were timber-clad. Smeared with orange mud and left to bake in the sun, the town was barely distinguishable from the bleak surroundings in which it stood.

Its sole *raison d'être* was due to its having grown up on a crossroads where trails snaked down from the pine-clad mountains to the north and south. Most travellers who partook of the town's limited facilities were prospectors who spent weeks dredging the mountain streams for paydirt. Quemado offered a respite from the endless toil.

Vance dumped the burro at the edge of town. The animal was just as keen to escape its brutal

80

master and the constant torment it had been forced to endure. Braying in triumph, it quickly darted away, disappearing behind a cluster of buildings. Good riddance, thought Vance shouldering his saddle-bags.

He ambled up the main street, eyes eagerly searching for an assay office. Exchanging the gold burning a hole in his pocket for good old US dollars was his first priority. Next on his list of essentials was a haircut and shave followed by a good soak in the bath, not to mention a proper meal; even after three days, he could still taste the vile concoction he had been forced to stomach back at the miners' camp.

Consequently it was evening before he decided to call it a day and retire to his room at the Imperial Palace. Advertised as the best hotel in town, it was in fact the only such establishment and not exactly boasting five star extravegence either. Indeed, it was little more than a rooming-house.

Which was why Vance decided to call in at the local saloon for a nightcap or three to counter the bed bugs that were doubtless lurking beneath the covers.

The Long Tom was well named. Meant as a reference to the Heath Robinson device aimed at removing gold from sleuced gravel, the room stretched back from the open street like a narrow corridor. A mahogany bar occupied the whole of one side with round tables down the other. A raised stage at the far end was clearly reserved for a band although no space was available for dancers to strut their stuff.

Dull sepia photographs of mining enterprises covered the walls. In contrast, a garishly colourful painting of a half-naked Amazon stared down on to the drinkers from behind the bar. Vance had spent much of his free time drinking in countless similar establishments, and instantly felt at home.

'What'll it be, stranger?' inquired the jovial host. 'First drink is always on the house. After that we charge double.' The rotund barkeep's ample girth shuddered with glee at his hilarious jocularity.

'Maybe I ought to have a bottle of the best,' grinned Vance joining in the merriment. 'That way I'm a winner all round.'

'Sorry, fella,' said the barman quickly reining in his over-zealous offer. 'It only applies to single shots.'

'And why don't that surprise me?' was the newcomer's mordant response. A hooked talon pointed to a bottle of red label behind the bar.

He grabbed the proffered bottle and sauntered over to an empty table. Being able to relax with a much needed injection of the hard stuff gave the killer chance to assess his options for the successful completion of his vendetta. Now that he had the opportunity to sit down and think things out, the true import of his undertaking lurched to the fore.

The deduction reached was that it would be no simple task.

The initial rush of bloodlust had faded to be replaced by a more circumspect appraisal. Not that he was any less thirsty for revenge, just more realistic as to its successful completion as a solo venture.

Eugene Vance was a dirt farmer, more at home with a ploughshare and scyth. Facing down a lethal and proven gunhand such as Lightning Cal Gentry would be like placing his hand in a rattler's nest.

The more he considered the situation, the more Vance was of the view that help was needed. The adage that you should fight fire with fire, or set a thief to catch a thief had merit. What he needed was another professional gun toter, someone to even out the odds and ensure a happy ending – for Eugene Vance at any rate.

He was seated at a table adjacent to some enclosed booths that were reserved for private discussions, business meetings and the like. Only one was occupied. Heavy red velvet drapes swathed the small cubicle, but Vance was still able to earwig the conversation being played out within.

Initially he displayed no interest. It was only when a single name was uttered by one of the hidden speakers that his attention was pricked.

Gentry!

Could it be the same guy? Had to be. What would these guys be wanting with that critter? Vance moved closer to the booth, placing his twitchy ear close to the drape. The muted voices were pitched low; they clearly didn't want to be overheard. But Vance was near enough to pick up the gist of the conflab.

'How do we know he's headed this way?' inquired a hard growling voice, roughened by too much hard liquor. Jeb Starkey was the oldest of the trio. 'Gentry always said he wanted to start up a spread raising prime Herefords,' replied a drawling Texas lilt.

'Yeah! He told me that as well,' interjected a third speaker. The crisp intonation implied the speaker to be on the youthful side. 'And I recall him mentioning that by going west he could find some place to settle down.'

A terse grunt of disdain greeted this suggestion.

'That's a mighty large hunk of territory, Kid,' rasped the first speaker. 'How in thunder are we supposed to find one guy out there?'

A pregnant silence enveloped the secret conclave.

It was the Texan who broke the tense quietude.

'We do know he's started calling himself Will Bennett. All we gotta do is keep dropping the name.'

'That's right!' cut in Kid Branson. 'There's gotta be some bartender who remembers a drifter with that handle.'

'Ugh!' grunted the oldest member of the group, hawking up a glob of baccy cud. 'A common enough handle. Could take us months of chasing up wild geese by the hundred afore we run him to earth.'

'I say we keep going and hunt down that double-crossing varmint for as long as it takes.' Tex Rammakin was adamant that he for one did not intend giving up the loot that Cal Gentry had stolen from them. He fixed the others with a defiant glare. 'Are we all agreed?'

A series of grunted affirmations greeted the challenge.

That was when their discussion was interrupted by a blunt snarl from the other side of the closed drape.

Vance had been so riveted by the screened discourse that he had failed to heed the approach of a fourth member of the gang. Only when the cold steel of a gun barrel jammed into his neck did he realize that listening in on a private parley was asking for an early burial.

'Perhaps you'd like to join me and my pards,' hissed an icy voice edged with menace. Refusal to comply was clearly not a healthy option. 'And explain how a nosey skunk happens to find our business so interesting.' The heavyweight Remington revolver's hammer snapped back. 'Now move it, ratface!'

The heavy drape was flung aside.

'What in tarnation is this?' ejaculated the startled Texan, quickly palming his own pistol.

'Looks to me like some snooper itching to have his hide ventilated,' snarled the weasel-faced hothead known as Kid Branson. The young gunman quickly hauled the alarmed snooper into the booth and slammed his quaking body into a vacant seat.

The older guy quickly scanned the elongated length of the saloon. Nobody appeared to have noticed the brief altercation. He gave a satisfied grunt before closing up the booth.

Four pairs of simmering eyes glowered at the unwelcome rubberneck.

'You better have a rock solid explanation for earwigging a private talk, fella.' Stoney faces nodded in acquiescence to Jeb Starkey's threatening comment. Four six-guns indicated the end result should the explanation prove less than convincing.

'Out with it!' snarled Rammakin. A lethal Bowie knife had appeared in his left hand. It tickled the intruder's bobbing Adam's apple nicking the skin. A thin drizzle of blood etched a trail down Vance's throat. 'Spill the grief. And it better be good.'

Vance tried desperately to avoid gulping.

'Hold on there, boys,' stuttered the quaking eavesdropper. 'It ain't what you think. It was the name of Gentry that caught my attention.'

'Why does Cal Gentry have so much interest for a nosey varmint like you?' demanded Clay Tarbuck. The loose-limbed hardcase had been fixing up some bunks for the night at the miners' dosshouse when he happened upon the shifty earwigger.

'He shot two of my brothers,' blurted out Vance eager to prove his bonafide credentials to these hardboiled rannies. 'Gunned 'em down in cold blood. Me and a cousin set out to seek revenge but poor old Bob never made it either. He was gunned down as well after we'd tracked Gentry to Socorro.'

Vance failed to mention that Connor had been shot while engaged in a piece of skulduggey that had come unstuck. Then his eyes assumed a rabid glint, a tentative smile edging out his initial nerves. This was where he could play a winning hand.

'I couldn't help overhearing that you boys seem to be wallowing in quicksand,' he said gently fingering aside the deadly blade at his throat. 'I was able to learn from the marshal in Socorro exactly where Gentry is headed.'

'And where might that be?' snarled the Kid.

Vance was about to divulge this vital piece of information when he realized this was his trump card. Once the gang knew that Gentry was bound for Safford in the Gila Valley, his life wouldn't be worth a plugged nickel.

'Now that'd be telling, boys,' he chirped. 'All I can tell you is that he's headed for Arizona.'

A growl of rage erupted from the Texan's throat. 'Why you double-dealing skunk.' The hand clutching the deadly blade rose to deliver the final *coup de grace.*

'Do that and you'll never find Gentry,' shot back the nervy dirt farmer knowing he was playing with fire and might end up getting his ass burned. The knife hovered in the still air, slivers of light from the tallow lamps glinting on the shiny steel. Vance hurried on, desperate to ease the tension and prove he had a winning hand. 'Let me come in with you fellas, and we can all come out on top.'

Starkey lifted a restraining hand to avert any precipitant action. The old reprobate recognized that their unannounced guest had a valid point. A dirt farmer judging by his stained dungarees, but he was no lunkhead. Once they had acquired that all-important final destination, the guy knew he would be surplus to requirements, a liability.

'Don't be so hasty, Tex,' chided Starkey. 'Mister . . . er?'

'V-Vance . . . Eugene V-Vance,' was the stuttered reply.

'Mister Vance here is only trying to protect his interests. Can't blame a guy for that, can you?'

'Guess not,' mumbled the less than convinced Texan hardcase.

'So Gentry's heading for Arizona,' muttered Starkey thoughtfully.

'What does he wanna go there for?' enquired a sceptical Clay Tarbuck.

'According to my information,' continued Vance who had regained his dented confidence now that the gang were giving his comments measured consideration, 'Gentry has bought some land down that way.'

Kid Branson butted in with a fervent confirmation of the newcomer's assertion. 'Didn't I tell you boys that the critter was headed west.'

'And I suppose it does fit with me knowing about his interest in raising Herefords,' added a grudging Tex Rammakin.

'So how about it, fellas?' asked the rejuvenated Eugene Vance. 'Don't it make sense that we join up?' He eyed the quartet of tough faces. 'Another gun will always come in handy when dealing with a sharp dude like Gentry.'

The gang cast hesitant looks at each other. Did they want another critter sharing in the loot once Gentry was taken care of? It was left to the wisdom of Jeb Starkey to make the final decision; by dint of age and experience the old guy had adopted the post of gang leader.

Vance saw the hesitation etched in the grim-faced

stares. His life hung in the balance here. So he pressed his case by assuring the gang they would be no worse off if he joined their ranks.

'I ain't asking for a share of the readies,' he affirmed with vigour. 'Once Gentry is pushing up the daisies, I can head back to Socorro and pick up the promised bounty from a certain lawdog who wants him out of the picture.'

'And who might that be?' inquired Starkey.

'Goes by the handle of Kansas Jack Tillman.'

Starkey's eyes lit up.

'So that jasper has deserted the owlhoot trail,' he murmured to himself.

The others threw him a flurry of puzzled looks.

'You know this critter, Jeb?' It was Clay Tarbuck who put their quandary into words.

'Sure do, boys,' said the old outlaw stoking up a corncob pipe. A languid smile crossed the weathered contours of his grizzled visage as a plume of smoke dribbled from between clenched teeth. 'Me and him rode together after the war. We joined up with Gentry in Abilene.' He shrugged at the recollection. 'He disappeared from the scene when the gang split up.'

Starkey paused to mull over this unexpected revelation. 'So the jigger has turned lawdog. I'd never have thought it.'

Vance remained on tenterhooks while the gang leader continued with his reminiscing.

'Gentry wasn't given the nickname of Lightning on account of his knowledge of the weather,' voiced the grizzled veteran. 'That guy is lethal with a six shooter as we all know.'

'Oftentimes, it feels like he's gotten eyes in the back of his head,' agreed Clay Tarbuck shaking his head. 'The guy's unbeatable.'

'And this dude can lead us to the exact spot,' said the Kid nodding towards Vance, 'which will save us a heap of time.'

'Then we're agreed,' said Starkey fixing them each with a meaningful regard. 'This guy's in.'

Nods all round.

Vance heaved a gentle sigh of relief.

'Much obliged, boys,' he said. 'You won't regret it.'

'If'n we do, you're dogmeat, mister,' snapped a flint-eyed Kid Branson.

Vance responded with a nervous laugh. 'You can depend on me,' he replied. 'So how's about we settle it with a drink.' A shaky grin accompanied the suggestion.

'Good suggestion, Eugene. And you're paying,' smirked the old bandit slapping the newcomer on the back. Then he added with a sly dig, 'For the rest of the night.'

'A gang tradition,' concurred Tarbuck winking at his buddies. 'Newest recruit always coughs up.'

A ribald series of hearty guffaws followed the newcomer as he swung out of the booth and headed over to the bar.

'So what's Gentry done that's gotten you boys so lathered up?' inquired Vance once he was seated back in the booth with his new sidekicks.

Grinning faces froze in a rictus of grim recall as their thoughts harkened back to that bleak day some two months previously.

NINE

TURNCOAT

The robbery had been carried off with cool preci-
sion. Everything had gone according to plan – a stark
contrast to the gang's previous heist where two men
had been killed and the take had been much less
than anticipated. This operation had netted enough
to keep the outlaws in clover for months.

Cal Gentry had planned it while drowning his
sorrows. He was sick of being constantly on the run
and wanted to quit the owlhooter trail. But it was not
that easy, so he had ended up in Great Bend's notorious Pawnee Saloon.

It was the nearest Kansas watering hole for the
troopers stationed at Fort Larned which sat on a
broad flat plain two hours' ride to the south-west. Cal
had got into conversation with a trooper whose vocal
output had become more boisterous as the bourbon
had disappeared down his throat.

Once he had learned that the guy was employed in the fort's main office, Cal had steered him away from the hullabaloo at the bar over to a more secluded corner.

Private Rick Johnson had been passed over for promotion on account of his slovenly appearance and habit of getting into fights. The gang leader couldn't help but smirk in agreement at the promotion board's decision: Johnson was certainly no advert for sartorial elegance. But, being employed in the company office, he did have access to vital information concerning payroll shipments.

It took little persuasion for a deal to be struck. Johnson, however, demanded payment for his services up front.

'How do I know you guys won't just disappear into the wide blue yonder once the dough has been seized,' challenged the glaring trooper. 'Then where would I be?' Johnson drew in his stomach and tossed another shot down his throat. 'In the doghouse, that's where. This way I can sneak off and start up afresh someplace else.' A dreamy cast softened the hard stubbly features. 'They tell me there's been a new gold strike up north in the Black Hills.'

No arguments as to his associates' trustworthiness would sway the bull-necked renegade. Under duress, Cal was forced to agree to the jigger's terms. His finances at the time were somewhat limited due to the spate of thin hauls. This deal would clean the gang out. But the payroll clerk had given the assurance that the rewards would be well worth the investment.

They agreed to meet up the following day once Cal had convinced the others that this was the caper that had all the makings of a winning hand.

The payroll wagon was coming south from Hayes City and would have to slow up once it had crossed the shallow waters of the Walnut. Only two soldier boys were escorting the wagon which had come south from the railroad depot by way of a little-known backtrail. A previous attempt, although unsuccessful, had made the camp commander wary of the main routes.

The robbery took place as the wagon was passing through a narrow rocky defile on the south side of the river.

It all happened in a split second. One minute the wagon was trundling along, the soldiers aimiably chatting together. The next, they were confronted by a gang of heavily armed gunmen hollering and threatening dire consequences should they display any resistance.

'Raise your hands and don't make no stupid moves,' rasped Gentry who had positioned himself on the crest of the rocky excrescence.

The others spurred out from behind the rocks and surrounded the wagon. A flight of meadow larks rose in fright at this sudden disturbance. A medley of clamorous twittering accompanied the harsh commands.

'Any thoughts about drawing those hoglegs and you're all dead meat,' sang out Kid Branson jabbing his revolver at the driver.

Prudence and a regard for their continued good health encouraged the bluebellies to comply with the blunt orders. Three pairs of hands grabbed for the clouds scudding by overhead.

'Now throw down that strongbox, pronto!'

The gang leader was on his feet, a Winchester jammed into his right shoulder covering the startled troopers. There was no hesitation. The heavy box dropped with a dull thud on to the ground.

'You won't regret it,' smiled the leader of the quartet. Scrambling down from his lofty perch, he blasted the padlock securing the loot. The contents brought a wide grin to his handsome features: there was more dough here than he'd thought.

Once it had been bagged up, Lightning Cal Gentry was feeling in a benevolent frame of mind. Displaying a measure of nonchalent aplomb, he handed the escort a reward for their welcome compliance.

'Just a little something to show our appreciation,' he said tapping his nose meaningfully. 'Best keep it to yourselves though. The other soldier boys at the fort might get jealous and start asking questions.'

'Much obliged, mister,' the driver replied ogling the wad of dough. It was more than he earned in two months. 'You won't get no trouble from us, eh fellas?'

The other two nodded eagerly, accepting their own rewards which were quickly pocketed as if they expected this surprise gift to be suddenly withdrawn.

Cal laughed. 'Don't worry, boys. I ain't gonna rob you a second time.'

That eased the tension.

Then. A quick slap on the rump of the lead horse, accompanied by whoops and yells from the robbers, and the wagon was sent careering off along the trail in the direction of Fort Larned. Cal scuttled back to the top of the rocky knoll, just to make certain the cavalrymen did not try any funny business. He would have hated to cut them down after the heist had gone off so smoothly.

The gang then spurred off heading west back to their hideout on the banks of Smoky Hill Creek.

What the rest of the gang did not know was that their leader had other plans for the payroll. Cal had resolved to put his notorious past behind him. Only then could he go in search of his wife and child to start afresh where his reputation would raise no eyebrows.

Unbeknown to the rest of the gang, he had contacted the state governor and agreed to hand over the proceeds of the robbery and let the authorities know where the gang could be apprehended. Only then would the slate be wiped clean. Also part of the agreement was that any wanted dodgers for Lightning Cal Gentry would be withdrawn.

He had arranged to pick up a letter of pardon once the dough had been handed over.

Nearing a deep ravine spanned by a trestle bridge, Cal made the excuse that his horse had picked up a stone in its hoof.

'You boy's carry on,' he said casually. 'I'll catch you up soon as I've dug it out.'

Unsuspecting that their leader was up to no good, the others pushed on across the bridge. As soon as they had disappeared from view, Cal removed two sticks of dynamite from his pack and set the charges under the edge of the main supporting beams. A twenty second fuse allowed him to find shelter behind some rocks.

When it came, the blast shook the ground making his ears ring. Shards of debris from the shattered bridge flew overhead. Not waiting for the dust to clear, he hurried over to the edge of the ravine, his taciturn demeanour cracking in a terse smile of satisfaction.

A yawning gulf more than twenty feet across told him that his ruse had succeeded. No way could the rest of the gang get back across the ravine. And the nearest crossing point of the chasm was a day's ride to the east. That afforded more than enough time for Cal Gentry to disappear and start a new life as Will Bennett.

It was only later that guilt began to prick at the reformed outlaw's conscience. The guys didn't deserve this. They had been a good bunch to ride with and deserved better. Monument Butte was where he had agreed to meet up with the posse led by a Pinkerton detective to hand over the loot. The guy would then give him that all important letter of pardon.

But the nearer he got to the soaring pinnacle of rock, the more Cal resolved to send the posse off on a wild goose chase.

Once they had discovered the subterfuge, it would be too late. Cal Gentry would have crossed the state border into Colorado.

What he hadn't reckoned with was the tenacity of his buddies, and their penchant to get even.

Eugene Vance helped himself to another shot of red-eye. Following the sombre revelations, he was more keen than ever to catch up with the double-dealing skunk. The guy was only perhaps three weeks ahead of them, and with his vital knowledge concerning the traitor's final destination, Vance was eager to get the job finished. Having learned about the loot his quarry was toting, the dirt farmer now had every intention of dipping his own fingers into the pie.

What the gang didn't know at this particular juncture was that it was all a chimera, a fantasy, and they were chasing a dream.

'He's driving a wagon,' said Vance, 'which will slow him down. 'Give us plenty of time to catch up. If'n we push it, he won't have chance to spend much of that lovely dough.'

'Gentry ain't gonna hand the loot over without a fight,' cautioned the Texan gunslinger, his thick eyebrows crinkling in alarm.

'Surely five of us ought to be able to handle one critter,' scoffed the Kid aiming a mocking eye at his faltering sidekick. 'Not scared are yuh, Tex?'

Rammakin leapt to his feet, angrily grabbing the smirking Kid by the throat. Gimlet eyes hard as lumps of coal pierced the simpering rannie. 'I'll take on any manjack that calls me out,' he raged, a rush of blood turning his face bright red. 'And that includes a tenderfoot whippersnapper like you. Remember that, Kid, else you ain't gonna see another daybreak.'

Branson's eyes popped. He knew that he had gone too far.

'Sorry, Tex,' he burbled. 'Just funning, is all.'

'Well don't! 'Cos it might be the last joke you crack,' replied Rammakin releasing his grip on the young tough. The Texan's volatile temper cooled down as quickly as it had blown up.

'One thing's been bugging me,' cut in the new recruit who had been enjoying the sudden flare up. Raised eyebrows told him he had their attention. 'You said there were four guys taking part in that last payroll heist.'

Starkey nodded.

'So how come there are still four of you now that Gentry has deserted?'

Tarbuck offered the query a curt laugh.

'Go on, tell him, Jeb.'

'After Gentry's double-dealing stunt, we hadn't got more'n a bent nickel between us. So when we'd crossed into Colorado, I figured we needed some quick readies.'

Starkey paused to re-kindle his pipe which gave the smirking Tarbuck chance to continue the story.

'We holed up on the main westbound trail between Lamar and Pueblo,' he explained. Plumes of acrid smoke from the corncob blending with the usual mix of sweat and stale beer made for a nause-ating mixture that might have overcome less hardened folk. Nobody appeared to notice. Neither a wrinkled snout nor a curled lip broke the intense concentration as Tarbuck drew breath.

On the far side of the dimly lit room, a band had struck up. Banjo, fiddle and jug combined in a spir-ited rendition of that famous old number, *Oh Suzannah!* Tarbuck was forced to raise his voice to be heard above the twanging cacophany.

'There was a constant stream of traffic,' he shouted keeping a wary eye open that his discourse remained covert, 'but nothing that was likely to net us a decent haul.'

'We'd almost given up.' Rammakin couldn't help jumping in with his own version of events. Starkey sat back and allowed him to continue. 'That's when a stagecoach came into view. And with no jasper riding shotgun, this was our chance. . . .'

'What we hadn't known was that it was special delivery. The passengers included a county sheriff and his prisoner.' A ribald chuckle emerged from the open mouth of the grinning Kid Branson. Rammakin ignored the interruption. 'Once the coach had reined up, we ordered the passengers outside.' He paused as all eyes focused on the sim-pering young buck. 'And guess who we found inside. . . ?'

'Not this dude?' exclaimed a startled Eugene Vance jabbing a thumb at the excited Kid.

Branson couldn't contain his mirth any longer.

'You got it, mister,' he cackled. 'And was I glad to meet up with these guys seeing as how I was headed for a stretch in the jail at Fort Bent – a little matter of getting caught breaking and entering a general store in Lamar. And when I found that the gang were one man down, I asked to be taken on.' He threw his arms wide with a raucous whoop. 'And here we all are.'

'What happened to the tinstar?' enquired Vance.

'Let's just say he didn't continue the journey to Fort Bent.'

Hard-boiled guffaws left Vance with no doubts as to the fate of the unfortunate lawman.

'All told, it was a good job,' concluded Starkey. 'The other passengers coughed up no less than five hundred bucks between them.' Pushing back his chair, the outlaw rose to his feet. 'If'n we want to catch up with Gentry lickety-split, then I suggest we get some shuteye and make an early start in the morning.' Then he addressed the newest recruit. 'You got someplace to stay, Vance?'

'I'll bed down in the livery.' He had purposely kept quiet about his own recent acquisition of funds. 'My pockets ain't exactly flush with dough at the moment. So if'n the place is good enough for my nag, its good enough for old Eugene too.'

TEN

LEAD POISONING AT GUTHRIE

The five men left Quemado hunkered beneath grey slickers, their hats pulled low over grim faces glistening with rainwater. A thunderstorm had broken soon after midnight and it was still going strong by first light. Jagged flashes shot across the sky illuminating the sorry huddle of adobe squats lining the rutted street.

Initial progess was slow due to the clinging mud, but at least the gang knew that this was the final stage of getting their revenge on their Judas ex-partner. Perhaps the scorching streaks rampaging across the Heavens was an auspicious sign of things to come.

Only time would tell. And they did not want to waste a minute of it.

The trail led south over the Tularosa Mountains then down the Frisco Valley to its junction with the

Gila. Not too far as the crow flies but a fatiguing strength-sapping route, especially for the horses which were forced down to little more than walking pace.

When anybody voiced a complaint, Starkey reminded them that Gentry would have had to take the longer route by way of Springerville and Oak Creek Canyon due to the wagon team he was driving. By taking this more ardous trail, they would save a week.

Three days out from Quemado and the bad weather finally broke. A stiff wind blew the bunched storm clouds away to the north allowing the welcome sun to make its presence felt. Saturated clothes soon dried in the heat, plumes of rising steam gave the riders the appearance of a giant cauldron.

Massed ranks of Ponderosa Pine and Douglas Fir blocked in the trail on all sides. Only when they climbed over the numerous ridges did the distant panorama open up only to reveal more of the same. Serated peaks with gnarled claws prodded at the azure fermament.

No other travellers had been encountered, and few wild creatures of the forest had been spotted apart from a lone deer that had provided a welcome relief from refried beans and sowbelly. The only other living things seen were occasional buzzards floating overhead on rising thermals.

Jeb Starkey kept up a relentless pace. After ten days on the trail, the tired group of riders descended the final tortuous trail into the Gila Valley. They stopped at the first settlement encountered – rest and recuperation were needed following the arduous mountain trek.

Guthrie was little more than a trading post complete with corrals, hay barn and a bunkhouse for weary travellers. The owner of the post had decided to name it after himself. A lurid signpost painted bright green announced that the gang had reached the town of Guthrie – Elevation: 3,250 feet, Population: three. Having a town named after him made Hank Guthrie feel important.

Tying up at the hitching post, the five trail-weary riders shouldered through a heavy oak door into the gloomy interior. Rough and ready was an apt description of the large room. Straw covered the dirt floor; Apache rugs and trophy heads of elk and grizzly bear covered the bare log walls. The bar was little more than a couple of planks supported by empty beer barrels.

The proprietor resembled a hungry bald eagle. His beaky snout pecked the air as he eyed the newcomers while scrubbing the bar top. They stood by the door surveying the less than congenial surroundings.

'What'll it be, fellas?'

The blithe inquiry was answered by five heads nodding towards a poster nailed to the wall behind the bar. Mammoth ribeye steaks smothered in fried potatoes and chilli sauce were judged to be a priority. It didn't matter that it was the only thing on the menu.

But first.

'Cold beers all round,' hollered the rasping voice of Jeb Starkey, his throat hoarse with trail dust. He coughed up a lump of grit and hawked the gunge on to the floor.

The proprietor was happy to oblige on both counts. He shouted their order to a room behind while pulling the beers.

'You boys heading far?' he asked slamming each tankard on to the bartop.

Before anybody could let slip their real intent, Starkey jumped in with a swift response.

'We're bound for Tombstone,' he averred firmly. 'Hear tell there's a mountain of silver been discovered down that way.'

'Sure has,' concurred the trader slapping the last drink on the bar. 'Biggest strike down this way. A fella by the name of Ed Shieffelin discovered it back in '77. Some reckoned the only sure thing to be dug out of the ground would be tombstones. And that's how the town got its name.' The guy's leathery face evinced a knowing smirk. 'They were sure right there. You boys be on your guard. That place is one wide open burg.'

'Just right for us then,' cut in Tarbuck nudging Rammakin in the ribs. Both men laughed uproariously. They were thoroughly enjoying the subterfuge.

'Sure is,' agreed Branson. 'Can't wait for some action after that trek over the mountains.'

It was Vance who decided to slip a casual inquiry into the general chitchat regarding their real intentions.

'Somebody told me that Safford was quite a big place,' he said gazing nonchalently at the array of patterned rugs lining the rough log walls.

'More a place for cattle breeders and the like,' replied Hank Guthrie.

The Kid sniffed.

'Not for the likes of us, eh boys?'

Shaking heads and muttered imprecations concurred with this assertion.

The gang retired to a corner of the room to discuss their next move. Silence descended over them as Guthrie arrived with their food.

'Bunks are a dollar a night if'n you want to stay over,' said the trader, laying their steaming plates on a table. 'Same for graining your mounts.' Then in a sly whisper, he added. 'And I've gotta a couple of willing Apache gals out back who can keep you company for a small extra charge.' The gaunt face leered down at his guests as he rubbed his grubby paws together.

'Much obliged,' replied Starkey barely able to contain a wry smirk as he laid a caustic peeper over the sorry specimens on offer. 'We'll take the bunks, and let you know about the erm . . . entertainment.'

As it happened, only the Kid chose to avail himself of the offer, much to the merriment of his sidekicks.

'This your first time?' joshed Vance, nudging Tarbuck while aiming a sly wink at Starkey.

' 'Course not,' bristled the young gunnie, squaring his shoulders. 'Had a half dozen or more.'

But the ardent remonstration lacked sufficient bounce. Coupled with a face tinted beetroot purple, it was abundantly clear to even a temperance maid that Branson was a total greenhorn in the bedroom stakes. One of the Apache squaws would have to make the running.

Next morning, the five travellers were awoken by a raucous hollering from a cockerel. Muttered grunts of complaint accompanied the lusty caterwauling. Kid Branson was the first to surface, a smile wider than the Grand Canyon creasing his youthful visage.

After a breakfast of corndogs and coffee, Guthrie ambled across and presented their bill.

'Hope you boys enjoyed your stay with us?' he said waiting expectantly.

'Sure did,' smiled Starkey. 'There's only one problem.'

Guthrie's response was a quizzical frown.

'You see, mister,' interjected Tex Rammakin shaking his head. 'We ain't got no way of paying you.'

'Flat broke,' from Tarbuck, who slapped his pockets expressively.

'Not a bent nickel between us,' was the Kid's adjunct to the bizarre powwow.

Hank Guthrie took a step back as he realized that these varmints had played him for a sucker.

'You scurvy dogs had this planned all along,' he protested, his voice raised in anger. 'Being all nice and friendly while aiming to rob me. Well two can play that game.'

Quick as a flash he dived behind the bar and grabbed for a loaded shotgun kept there for just such an emergency as this. The sudden move took the gang by surprise. Guthrie had the gun raised and was thumbing back the twin hammers before they were able to draw their own weapons.

Before anybody could open fire, a knife took Branson in the shoulder. It had been thrown by Little Dove, the squaw who had deflowered the Kid during the previous night. He yelped, more in shock than from the pain. That would come later. Staggering back, he slumped to the floor clutching at the hilt of the heavy blade.

That was when all hell broke loose.

Gunfire erupted. Orange flames spurting from four revolvers synchronized with the deep boom of the shotgun blast. White smoke from pistol shells mingling with the black powder of shotgun cartridges blurred the gruesome tableau. And the noise was deafening. The gun battle ended almost before it had begun. In total, it had lasted for no more than twenty seconds.

At the end of the lethal exchange Guthrie lay dead, slumped across the bartop, blood dripping from a dozen bullet wounds. One of his Indian squaws had likewise been taken out by shots in the stomach and chest. She was still alive, but only just. Her sister, who had wisely kept her head down during the short yet brutal conflict, dragged her behind the counter.

But the gang had not escaped unscathed either. Clay Tarbuck would not be continuing the ride to Safford. The twin blasts of Guthrie's shotgun had taken his head clean off. It was not a pretty sight, a shattered hunk of bone and sinew rolling about in the straw.

Over in a corner, the Kid was howling in pain.

'Cut the belly-aching,' growled Starkey taking a firm grip of the knife hilt jutting from the bleeding shoulder. 'You're making more noise than that darned rooster.'

A swift tug and the glinting blade slid free with a sickening glug. Exhibiting a less than charitable concern, Starkey brusquely assured the whining brat that he would live. He untied the Kid's bandanna and stuffed it into the bleeding wound.

'Keep a hold of this until we find a sawbones to stitch you up,' he snapped. Starkey adjudged that it was time to leave. All that gunfire might well attract unwelcome attention. He snapped out an order to Vance.

'Bring the nags round to the front.'

The dirt farmer nodded then scurried away over to the barn.

Within three minutes he was back.

'All set, boss,' he called through the open door.

Starkey backed towards the door keeping his gun levelled on the surviving Apaches. 'Ok boys, let's get out of here.'

The others needed no encouragement to follow. All were anxious to leave the brutal scene of carnage.

Only Rammakin had the foresight to reach behind the bar and dip his hand into the safe, conveniently left open, where the trader kept his dough. A smile of satisfaction accompanied the removal of a thick wad of greenbacks. Leaping into the saddle, he soon caught them up.

The four survivors of the bitter conflict galloped away, manic yells and their quirts urging the mounts to maximum speed. At that moment, distance from the macabre scene of death took precedence over all else.

Within five minutes they reached a junction in the trail. A weathered signboard pointing west read *Safford – twenty miles.* The trail south led to Tombstone. Starkey filed the information away in the back of his mind. Maybe when they had got even with Gentry, he would head down that way and check out the silver strike.

The gang left the main trail when they were about an hour's ride from Safford. Starkey's aim was to locate a good place to establish a camp that was unlikely to be spotted. A box canyon displaying no passage of people or animals was the type of place he was seeking.

'Keep your eyes peeled, boys,' he said after telling the others what to look out for. 'We need to find somewhere that nobody's gonna happen across except by accident.'

They had split up and agreed to meet back on the edge of the bluffs two hours hence. Only the Kid was allowed to rest up due to his wound which had started to bleed again.

Eventually it was Rammakin who stumbled across the ideal location. He couldn't wait to break the good news when the others finally returned to their rendezvous.

'It's two miles down this canyon, boss,' he stressed eagerly pointing back the way he had come. 'There's a side draw. I almost missed it. The entrance is covered by a clump of juniper trees. A couple of skulking coyotes drew my attention when they came out. It should make the perfect hideout.'

'What we waiting for then,' yipped Starkey spurring off with Rammakin leading the way. 'Let's go get us a hideyhole!'

After pushing through the tree cover, they emerged into a narrow ravine. Ten minutes later it opened up into a broad swathe of pastureland. There was even an abandoned line cabin abutting the far wall of fractured rock.

'Perfect!' enthused Starkey dismounting to inspect their new abode.

Once established, Kid Branson was ordered to head for Safford.

'Get the croaker to fix up at that gash,' said Starkey. 'Then find out if Gentry and his crew have arrived.'

'How am I gonna do that?' queried the Kid, his face grimacing at the pain from his injured shoulder.

A sigh of frustration issued from Starkey's clenched teeth.

'Who is the one dude in any town that knows everything?'

Branson's response was a blank stare of ignorance.

'The bartender, you numby,' rapped out the Texan.

'Oh, yeh,' drawled Branson mounting up.

'And make sure you tell the sawbones that the knife wound was an accident.' Starkey laid emphasis on this latter course as the Kid made to leave.

ELEVEN

UNEXPECTED ENCOUNTERS

The doctor's surgery was located on the edge of Safford. It was a neat two storey wooden building with a flower garden out front surrounded by a white fence. Branson was the only patient. The wound showed no signs of infection and was quickly dressed.

'Rest up in here awhile, young fella,' he said. 'Good job you came in to have that wound fixed. Had it been left unattended much longer, gangrene would have set in. And that would have meant the loss of your arm.'

Branson shivered. 'Much obliged, Doc,' he muttered.

The Kid was then left alone in the clinic while Doc Hobley attended to another patient who had just arrived.

While taking stock of his surroundings, Branson noticed a bottle labelled chloroform. He knew it was used to knock people out before operations. His pa had mentioned having had it administered while his leg was being amputated during the war. Not the sharpest knife in the box, the Kid nonetheless recognized that it might prove useful in the future. Gunshot wounds and other such injuries were an occupational hazard for outlaw gangs.

The bottle rapidly disappeared into his pocket just as the medic returned.

'That will be three dollars, please,' he said. 'And here's a spare dressing just in case that wound starts bleeding again.'

The Kid willingly paid up, then quickly left.

His next port of call was the biggest saloon in town. The Saddle Tramp occupied a prime site on the main street. It sure displayed all the trappings of a hellsapoppin' hotspot. A large wooden saddle overhung the front veranda and leaning out of the upstairs windows, a line of smirking calico queens openly advertised the quality of their wares.

The Kid's eyes stood out on stalks. This was just the kind of place he was seeking. He shouldered through the door and sashayed up to the bar. Starkey had impressed upon him that discretion and a low profile were vital for their mission to succeed.

Normally outgoing and garrulous, Branson forced himself to stay in the background. Remaining unnoticed and inconsequential was anethema to his usual style. And it rankled.

After ordering a drink, he casually asked the bartender if a tall stranger had arrived in town recently driving a wagon and with a wife and child in tow.

The 'keep gave the questioner a snooty frown.

'And who wants to know?' he sniffed imperiously.

The Kid felt like dropping him, but maintained his cool.

'He's my brother,' he breezed offering a leery grin. 'We're meant to be building up a spread in the valley.'

That seemed to satisfy the barman.

'You must be referring to Will Bennett,' he proferred. 'He lives down the street above the shop his wife has opened up.'

'I'm obliged,' replied Branson. 'Can I buy you a drink?'

That offer certainly opened the guy's mouth. By the time the Kid left an hour later, he was in possession of all the facts he required. Much as he would have preferred to linger over a few more drinks, and maybe sample one of those luscious dames upstairs, he deemed it wise to head back to the hideout. Plenty of time for that when they had pocketed the dough.

The pounding of hoofs brought the remaining gang members hurrying out of the cabin. Guns palmed, they skewered the rider with caustic frown. Only when they recognized the lean figure of Kid Branson did they relax.

The boy brought his mount to a skidding halt then

114

leapt deftly from the saddle. The acrobatic display did nothing for the wizened figure of Jeb Starkey. He was too long in the tooth for such flamboyant demonstrations.

'What did yuh find out?' he rasped in irritation. 'We ain't got time for no fancy tricks.'

Branson uttered an aggrieved snort. Ignoring the demand, he ambled over to the old well and vigorously pumped the arm. Once the water was flowing, he stuck his head under the spout. The sudden gush helped cool him down after the dusty ride.

'Come on, Kid!' hollered the impatient outlaw. 'We ain't got all day.'

Branson shook his dripping mane of blond locks before replying.

'We've sure come to the right place,' he declared enjoying the gang's undivided attention. 'A tall rangy guy calling himself Will Bennett has taken over the Bar BQ spread ten miles south of Safford.'

'That must be Gentry!' interjected Rammakin acidly.

Branson ignored the interruption. 'He's living above a dressmaker's shop that his wife has opened up. Their kid attends the local school. According to the bartender at the Saddle Tramp Saloon, this dude has spent each day out at the ranch repairing the place to make it habitable as a family home.'

'Urm!' Starkey twiddled the ends of his moustache in thought. 'Now all we gotta figure is how best to make him hand over the loot. Any ideas, boys?'

Pensive frowns followed as the outlaws got their

brains around the problem.

It was Tex Rammakin who offered the solution that would force the renegade's hand.

They thrashed out the details and arranged to make their play the following afternoon. The boy would be at school and Gentry would be at the ranch, leaving the girl alone in the shop.

'No way will that critter allow his dame to come to any harm,' remarked an upbeat Kid Branson.

'Yuh sure right there,' agreed a jubilant Jeb Starkey slapping the Kid on the back. 'This caper oughta be a piece of cake.' Then turning to Rammakin added, 'Good figuring, Tex.'

A bottle was passed around the smouldering embers in the stone grate. Smokes were ignited. All in all, it was a satisfying end to the day.

Long shadows were fast enveloping the hidden canyon as the sun shrank behind the rimrock. An owl hooted over to their left. The mournful sound was followed by a pinched squeal of fright as the gang settled down for the night. They would need an early start in the morning.

The steady rap of a hammer nailing on roof shingles bounced back from the two hundred foot cliff rising out of the San Carlos Flats behind the ranch house. To the side was a barn, its large door hanging askew on one hinge. Many of the wooden side panels were broken. On the other side of the main house, the corral was likewise in need of repair.

Ever since he had arrived in the Gila Valley two

weeks previously, Cal Gentry had been making a concerted effort to renovate the near derelict ranch house. He had bought the spread unseen from a land speculation brochure back in Nebraska. Now he understood why the price had been so low. What had at the time seemed like a bargain now transpired to be a chunk of scrubland complete with buildings that had seen much better days.

But at least it was his, and he had the deed of sale to prove it. More to the point, there was no mortgage owing to any money grabbing banker.

The reformed outlaw stretched his aching muscles and surveyed the extent of his property. It would need a heap of work to make for a viable concern. But Cal was an optimist. After coming to terms with the derelict nature of the property, he was well pleased with his purchase and couldn't wait to get started.

His first job had been to dig out the source of spring water from the well which had become blocked up through lack of use. Next was the roof; part of it had collapsed allowing rain to invade the interior of the building. There was a heap of other work to be done as well before he could even consider buying cattle to populate the range.

He had been working every hour of daylight to make the place habitable so that Cecelia and little Joe could have a decent place to live. In the meantime, they were renting a couple of rooms above the premises in Safford where his wife was trying to re-establish herself in the dressmaking business. It was

117

cramped but would suffice until the ranch was habit-able. That would take at least another couple of weeks.

Cal wiped away the sweat from his brow: it was hot work for a man unused to manual labour but he was enjoying every second. Unscrewing the cap from his water bottle, the ex-gunslinger took a long swig.

Another half hour and he would call it a day. It was Wednesday and he figured an early finish had been earned. Cecelia would have his lunch on the table when he got back to town. After all these years a mundane, some might say boring, life was all he wanted.

At long last, things appeared to be going in the right direction. He had put his guns away and prayed they would never again need to be used in anger. The novice rancher smiled. Tomorrow, he would reg-ister his Bar BQ brand with the local cattlemen's association under the name of Will Bennett.

That would be a proud moment indeed.

But Lightning Cal Gentry was not alone.

He was under observation from a solitary rider concealed behind a tangle of chaparal. The man closely watched the greenhorn cowboy. A nervy bearing had made the palms of his hands damp with sweat – not the actions of a jasper intent on causing trouble for the new rancher.

Kansas Jack Tillman had ridden hard and fast from Socorro.

He had only just arrived and heaved a quiet sigh of

relief that he was not too late. Tillman knew the territory like the back of his hand. He had hoped that by taking the longer route through Silver City and over the Peloncillo Mountains, he could overtake Eugene Vance and warn his old buddy of the danger he faced.

It had taken three days for the guilty conscience to build into a festering cancer that proceeded to eat away at the lawman's very soul. And all for what? Because he hankered after a women who had eyes only for one man. Jealousy had consumed his reasoning – blotted out all the good times they had once shared riding together.

The fact that Cal Gentry had saved his life on more than one occasion counted for nought when the green-eyed monster raised its ugly head.

So what was he going to do about it?

Matt Allison pushed open the door and sauntered into the office. He was Tillman's new deputy. The marshal had pressed the town council for extra assistance following the recent influx of unruly miners. The gun battle in which he had been forced to shoot down Rowdy Bob Connor had forced the issue.

Allison removed his hat and tossed it at the stand in the corner. It spun like a flying plate and settled perfectly on to the hook.

The deputy smiled.

He was something of a show-off and had not been Tillman's first choice. But being the mayor's son had its perks, and the prestigious appointment as deputy marshal had raised Matt's game substantially with the local *señoritas*.

Tillman usually regarded such displays with irritable disdain, but on this occasion he barely noticed the deputy's arrival.

'All quiet so far, Jack,' said the harebrained youngster. 'D'yuh want me to go question the Burton kid about that broken window in the church?'

Silence. Tillman was hugging a glass of whiskey. Bit early in the evening, mused Allison frowning.

'What about that broken window?' repeated the deputy, raising his voice.

'Ugh?' grunted Tillman taking another sip of the amber nectar and suddenly realizing he was not alone.

'The broken window!' snapped Allison. 'Don't yuh reckon it needs investigating?'

The marshal ignored the cutting invective of his subordinate. Without warning, he lurched to his feet and stepped over to the locked gun rack. Selecting a Winchester, he checked the load before strapping on his gunbelt.

'Where you going, Jack?' queried the bemused deputy. His senior's behaviour was becoming increasingly bizarre.

'You're in charge for the next four weeks,' he said with resolute determination. 'Think you can handle it?'

'S-sure, Jack,' stuttered the wide-eyed kid. 'Why are you in such an all-fired hurry? And where are you going?'

'Important business that can't wait,' blustered the lawman setting his hat straight. His stoney face set like a carved statue. 'Anybody asks, tell 'em its about that stage robbery near Magdalena. Got that?'

The bewildered younger man could only nod absently. Before his boss could leave, the deputy voiced a warning. He held up a wire that had just been sent over from the telegraph office.

'Watch out for a Chiricahua buck called Geronimo. It says here that him and a number of renegades have busted out of the San Carlos Reservation and are fixing to cause trouble.' Allison gave his boss a warning look. 'Heard tell that he's one mean dude.'

Tillman absently nodded his thanks. But his mind was elsewhere. The information was filed away at the back of his mind and instantly forgotten.

Within ten minutes of exiting the law office, Kansas Jack was spurring off down the street out of Socorro. He was travelling light: no pack mule, just a bedroll and saddle-bag stuffed with hardtack and beef jerky.

The journey had been uneventful until he had reached the trading post known as *Guthrie's Place.* The first thing he had noticed was an Apache squaw standing over a heap of stones that looked mighty like a grave. Her buckskin clothing was stained with blood intimating that bad business was afoot.

Tillman drew his pistol. All looked quiet. But in such circustances, it always paid to err on the side of caution. The girl turned as he approached. She was young, no more than sixteen years going on thirty.

'Speak English, girl?' inquired the lawman curtly.

The girl nodded.

'What happened here?'

'White eyes come through two days ago,' she said, tears forming in her red-rimmed eyes. 'Shot my sister. She lasted until this morning, then. . . .' The final utterance was too painful to complete.

Tillman stiffened.

'How many?'

'Five. Gang refused to pay for services. Little Dove knifed the yellow hair who had her night before. Sister say he like animal. The one who called himself Jeb Starkey killed Guthrie.' The girl spat in the dust. 'Best thing for that snake in the grass.' The retort was sharp and cutting.

Starkey! murmured Tillman under his breath. So that guy was still up to his old tricks. Last he heard, the outlaw was operating up in Nebraska. So what was he doing this far south?

'You alone here?' posed the white man.

'Yes.'

'Then I'd better escort you back to your tribe.' It was taking him out of his way. But he couldn't leave her here. 'What's your name?' he asked.

Wind That Sings, it turned out, was the youngest daughter of the legendary Apache warrior Geronimo. A blue-blooded squaw to be sure.

Tillman was impressed. He was also nervous. The brutal reputation of the Indian chief of the White Mountain Apaches was known and feared throughout the West. She revealed that Guthrie had bought them from some Mexican bandidos six months before.

A pained shout jerked the lawman back to his current situation. He couldn't resist a brief smile. It was only Cal sucking the thumb he had just hammered. Then he gulped hard. This was the moment he had been dreading.

But Cal deserved the truth. Only then could they both decide how best to thwart the attempted bushwacking that was imminent.

Tillman stepped into the open.

Seeing his old sidekick beavering away in a concerted effort to fashion a new life made the aging lawdog realize he had done the right thing. He sucked in a deep breath and began walking slowly towards the novice rancher.

Cal remained unaware that he was alone until a voice addressed him.

'You missed one,' remarked Tillman, his throaty utterance trying to inject a note of levity into the surprise intrusion.

Cal swung round, almost losing his balance.

His mouth dropped open. The sudden and unexpected appearance of his one-time partner had taken him aback. It registered in the startled response. 'What in tarnation are you doing here, Jack?'

'It's a long story, old buddy,' muttered the newcomer. 'Come down and we can talk about it.' Tillman paused unsure how to continue. 'It won't make for easy listening.'

Cal's face hardened, a grim expression replacing the gaping stare of seconds previously. He climbed down off the roof, the sore thumb forgotten as his pointed gaze fastened on to the twitchy lawman.

'I'll make us some coffee while you tell me what's going on,' he rasped hustling into the spartan interior of the ranch house.

Tillman followed more slowly. He lit up a smoke and sucked hard on the quirley. He was thinking hard about how best to put his abrupt arrival into words. They sat down on a pair of rickety old chairs facing each other.

Cal waited. Then the starpacker launched into his prepared dialogue.

He was not wrong about it being tough listening, but Cal allowed him to finish without interruption. As the sorry tale unfolded the listener's face quickly assumed a venomous slant. A lazy eye twitched as repellent anger threatened to burst out. Striding back and forth across the room, boots echoing on the bare floorboards, he struggled to retain control of his actions. Only when the nervous lawman had finished did he return to his seat.

Nothing was said for five minutes as the import of the parley sunk in.

It was hard to swallow. Outside a door banged. Both men jumped to their feet and dashed outside but it was only the wind.

Another five minutes passed with Cal Gentry staring blankly at the bare walls. The silence was too much for Tillman: he hung his head.

'Go on, punch me if'n you feel the need,' he moaned. 'Land sakes, I sure deserve it.'

'You ain't wrong there, mister.'

Cal's response was brittle and full of anger. But he remained seated. A dark cast lined the stolid features as he continued to ponder his companion's disclosure, and more important, what to do about it. He had not managed to survive all this time by panicking when things went awry.

Much as he felt like taking up his old partner's offer of beating the critter to a pulp, Cal appreciated the courage and grit it had taken for Kansas Jack to ride all this way to assuage his iniquity. And there was no denying that he could sure use the guy's help.

Vance might decide to take him out from an ambush. No way would it be a frontal challenge like before. The varmint could even be out there now, watching, awaiting his opportunity. Once again Cal walked over to the window and warily peered out, scanning the terrain. Only the gentle roll of tumble-weed disturbed the tranquil scene.

Then it struck him. Cecelia was alone. An hour's ride away in Safford. She could be in dire peril. Vance might decide to get at him through her. That conviction precipitated a curt response.

'Let's ride, Jack,' he said. 'Vance is around here some place and I need to get back to town, pronto!'

Tillman nodded as they hustled outside and mounted up.

TWELVE

GRIM DISCOVERY

The lathered horses were steaming as the two riders galloped headlong down the main street of Safford. Pedestrians were forced to jump aside and a variety of lurid curses followed the charging riders. But Cal Gentry had eyes only for the shop at the far end of town.

What would he find? Had Vance already made his odious presence felt?

The two riders drew to a shuddering halt in a welter of dust and indignant snorts from their driven mounts.

Leaping out of the saddle, Cal slammed into the shop.

It was empty.

'Cecelia! Cecelia!' he yelled. 'Are you there, honey?' The panic-stricken voice crackled with anguish.

There was no reply. Maybe she had just stepped out for a spell. But the place was in a mess. Rolls of cloth strewn around, balls of wool on the floor, chairs upended. And that smell. His nosed wrinkled. Then it struck him: they had used chloroform to subdue her.

He was about to return to the street when he noticed a piece of paper lying face up on the counter. It was pinned down by a large darning needle.

He grabbed hold of the missive. His face registered grievous despair as the contents struck home with the force of a blacksmith's hammer. The colour drained from his tanned features, replaced by the grey waxy pallor of death. Once again he read the awful meaning of what had occurred, mouthing the hateful words aloud.

'We've taken the girl. She ain't hurt. But it's up to you whether that remains so. Bring the dough that you stole from us after the Nebraska payroll heist to Warbonnet Rock and you can have her back unharmed. Be there by noon tomorrow and come alone. Pull any fancy tricks and she gets carved up.'

The note was signed by each member of the old gang. Jeb Starkey, Tex Rammakin, Kid Branson . . . and Eugene Vance. So that varmint had somehow joined them. He'd never heard of this Branson jasper. The Kid must have been taken on as a replacement after their old leader pulled the double-cross.

'Bad news?' inquired the tentative voice of Jack Tillman.

Without replying, Cal handed him the note.

A dour expression tinged with fear ranged across the lawman's leathery visage. The marshal now realized why Jeb Starkey had come to Arizona. His body tensed, waiting for the outburst of anger that would be coming his way.

Sure, Cal was angry, worried, distraught. A whole gamut of emotions flooded his addled brain. But he was thinking straight and his anger was not directed towards his old buddy. How could he turn this calamity around?

'I should have known that escape from the past was impossible,' he muttered, half to himself. 'Jeb Starkey was never going to just turn over and have his belly scratched like a flea-bitten mutt. Trouble is . . .' He paused as the true significance of his dilemma struck home, 'there ain't no dough. I handed it back to the authorities. And any money I had stashed away has gone to buying the Bar BQ and doing the place up.' He shrugged helplessly. 'There's nothing left.'

Tillman gave the troubled delivery a quizzical frown. Gingerly he laid a comforting hand on his old partner's shoulder.

'You want to tell me about the Nebraska job?' he asked.

'It was after your time,' replied Cal. 'The old gang had split up. . . .' He swallowed. His voice was flat, deadpan, but at least the anger had faded as the ex-gunfighter's pragmatic personality struggled to find a way forward.

Maybe talking it through would provide an answer.

Tillman led the hunched figure out of the shop and over to the nearest saloon. A drop of hard liquor was needed to calm shredded nerves.

'What am I gonna do, Jack?' muttered the unhinged man following his narrative. 'Those turkeys ain't kidding when they threaten dire retribution.' He threw his arms wide in helpless dismay. Another glass of bourbon slid down his throat. 'There's no way I can raise anything like the dough they're wanting except by robbing another bank.'

Tillman gave that suggestion a twisted grimace.

Cal offered his buddy a thin smile. 'Don't worry,' he opined. 'I ain't about go back down that road. There has to be another way.' He stared into the glass hoping that some miracle would appear out of the blue.

It did. But not from that direction.

Jack Tillman's sharp brain had been juggling with potential solutions to his *amigo*'s plight – he owed him that much. It was his fault that the old gang, together with Vance, now held all the aces and were threatening terminal consequences for 'Cecelia should his buddy fail to show up with a hefty wad of greenbacks.

A resolute glint showed in the lawman's narrowed gaze.

'Maybe I can come up with the solution to this mess,' he offered dragging the half empty bottle from a grasping hand. Cal swore. 'And it won't be found in a glass of hooch.'

'What are you getting at?'

'Listen up and I'll explain,' Tillman snapped back.

He waited until his associate had simmered down and was paying full attention before outlining the plan. 'Instead of ready cash, which ain't available,' he enthused, 'you offer to help them rob the monthly transfer of dough to the local bank's head office in Bisbee. Don't matter if there is no such delivery. The gang won't know that. If they figure it to be an easy haul, how can they refuse? It's either that or losing out completely. A dead girl is no use to a bunch of outlaws. You with me?'

Cal gave a perfunctory nod. The bottle was ignored as he thoughtfully digested the scheme. He was willing to try anything if it would get Cecelia back unharmed.

'I can square it with the county sheriff,' continued the galvanized tinstar. 'Persuade him to supply a stage crammed with armed deputies. Starkey and his boys are bound to have prices on their heads.' He paused to enable his buddy to consider the scheme. 'So what do you say?'

'One thing that don't fit right,' Cal reciprocated. 'Once these guys have been caught, that still leaves Cecelia in their clutches. And we don't know where they're holding her. They would still have the whip hand.'

His head drooped on to his chest after concluding they were no further along the road to getting her back. But Tillman had that eventuality covered.

'We let one of the gang escape, then follow him.'

For a second Cal remained locked in despair.

Then slowly, his head lifted. A new spark of hope flickered over the ashen landscape of his gaunt features.

'It might just work,' he whispered. It was nought but a hoarse croak.

'No might about it, old buddy,' urged Tillman fervently. 'Them fellas'll fall for the scheme hook, line and sinker. You can bet on it!'

After thrashing out the nitty gritty of the plan, Cal realized that he would need to arrange temporary accommodation for his son. The local school ma'am had become friendly with Cecelia. He was sure that she would oblige.

'Don't tell her about our plans,' cautioned Tillman. 'This has to be kept under wraps. No telling who could find out if it became public knowledge.'

They stood up to leave the saloon. Cal tapped the cork into the bottle of bourbon and returned it to the barman.

'Keep it under the counter, Charley,' he said. 'We might have some'n to celebrate in a couple of days.'

Out in the glaring light of late afternoon, Tillman headed for the marshal's office down the street, while Cal made his way in the opposite direction towards the school house.

Warbonnet Rock was a huge chunk of orange sandstone weathered into the shape of an Indian chief's headdress. The gang had chosen such a meeting place with care: there was no chance of any hidden bushwackers being able to jump them once the

131

money was exchanged.

The soaring landmark was isolated and surrounded by dry flatlands swathed in clumps of saltbush, catclaw and mesquite. Only the most hardy creatures could survive in such harsh surroundings. Most notable were the venomous Gila Monster and the chuckawalla lizard, not forgetting the deadly rattlesnake.

But of human settlement there was none.

Once he had established that Gentry was alone, Jeb Starkey led his men out from the cover of the Warbonnet. No effort was made to replay old times, no greeting from old buddies. Cal felt a dribble of sweat trickling down his neck and it was not due to the heat.

The two adversaries sat their horses facing each other no more than twenty feet apart.

'You got the money, Gentry?'

The demand was brusque and straight to the point.

But there was no money. The declaration received howls of indignation. Angry scowls threatened all manner of retribution.

'I oughta gun you down here and now,' growled the old gunman. 'What sort of skunk runs out on his partners like you did.'

'Let me do it, Jeb,' snarled Rammakin waving his revolver.

'Do that and you'll get nothing,' Cal stressed, quickly outlining his plan.

It had taken forceful persuasion and all of his

ingenuity to bring Starkey round to the belief that the plan to hold up the bank delivery was the only viable option.

'It's the only way,' shouted Cal. 'And didn't you boys ever stop to wonder how you never found a posse on your tails?' He jabbed a thumb at his chest. 'That was on account of me sending them off up north hunting for ghosts. I needed to start a new life, get rid of that reputation. The only way was to hand over the loot. They wanted you boys as well.'

'And you figure we should be grateful. Is that it?' Starkey hawked a lump of spittle at the notion. 'Steal our dough, then try to sweeten your blamed conscience. Well it don't work that way, mister. No sirree!'

'Don't it make sense though, Jeb,' pressed Cal. 'This one job and you boys will be in clover, set up for life.'

'Seems to me that I've heard that afore,' grumbled Rammakin.

'Well this time it's true,' returned Cal vigorously.

Starkey twisted the ends of his moustache in thought. Should he trust this turkey? In truth, he had no choice if they were to come out of this with anything to show for their trouble.

'OK, Gentry,' he announced. 'You got a deal. But just remember. If'n you pull a fast one this time, you'll never see that pretty head alive again.'

'Where you holding her?'

'Kid Branson is taking good care of her in a place you'd never find in a million years. It was only by accident we stumbled across it. The perfect hideout.' A broad grin of triumph splashed across the grizzled jasper's blotchy face.

Cal suppressed the urge to go for his gun. He could have removed that odious smirk with ease. But that way would surely lead to an unwelcome date with the Devil.

And so the plan was set in motion. The robbery was arranged for three days hence. Cal stifled a smile of his own.

Now all he had to do was bait the trap.

THIRTEEN

HOLD-UP AT WARBONNET

Cal had arranged to leave a message informing the gang of the exact time that the supposed bank delivery was due to pass by Warbonnet Rock. It was concealed beneath a conspicuous stone on the side of the trail.

On the appointed day, he had ridden out of Safford before sun up to rendezvous with Starkey and his boys.

'We've got half an hour before the wagon arrives,' he said after consulting the watch in his vest pocket. 'Time enough for a cigar.'

'There'll be no smoking until this caper has been pulled successfully,' rasped Starkey, fastening a bleak eye on to the Judas in their midst. 'Your days of bossing this outfit are over, Gentry. I'm in charge now.'

'Sure thing, Jeb,' Cal apologized replacing the cigar in his pocket. 'You're in charge. The money is all your'n. All I want out of this is my wife returning safely.'

'And so she will if you're on the level,' warned the new gang leader. 'But play us for suckers again and both of you are goners.'

Cal noticed that Starkey had brought along an extra hand. That must be the mysterious Kid Branson. He could see from the youthful cockiness that the Kid was a lethal blend of gun-hungry madcap recklessness. Not the sort of critter to inspire confidence as the guardian of his beautiful wife. The gunfighter shuddered to think what manner of abuse the poor girl had been subjected to.

So what had they done with her?

'Who's taking care of Cecelia?' His query was edged with trepidation.

It was the Kid who proffered the answer by producing a small bottle.

'This stuff sure is the bee's knees for sending someone to sleep,' he chortled.

'She better be alright!' warned Cal gritting his teeth.

'Don't worry none,' mollified Starkey, reading his old partner's mind. 'She ain't been touched if that's what's worrying you.'

Vance had been keeping watch on the trail.

'They're coming,' he called from atop a low mound of rocks.

The plan was to allow the wagon to pass the Rock

136

unmolested. Then the gang would emerge from cover and gallop after it on both sides. They would have no trouble overtaking a cumbersome wagon pulled by two horses.

'Take cover, boys,' hissed Starkey drawing his pistol. 'Anybody tries to resist, shoot them down.'

Cal's blood ran cold. He had no wish for any of the hidden deputies, nor the driver to get hurt. In the silence that followed, his heart pounded in his chest like a steam pump.

Then he heard it, the gentle tapping of shod hoofs and jingling traces getting louder as the wagon approached. A plume of ochre dust and then it thundered past. The high wooden sides were covered by a tarpaulin underneath which were the concealed defenders.

'Let's go, boys!' hollered Starkey digging spurs in his mount's flanks. Guns drawn the five hidden robbers dashed out from their place of concealment, Starkey and Rammakin on one side, Branson and Vance on the other with Cal bringing up the rear.

As soon as they drew level with the wagon, the tarp was thrown back and half a dozen heads appeared above the protective sides. Without any warning they began firing.

Realizing he had been taken for a fool, Starkey immediately backed off and aimed his revolver at the source of his frustration. A warped smile split the craggy profile as Cal Gentry threw up his hands and tumbled from the saddle.

Seeing his nemesis out of action, the gang leader

dragged his horse around and galloped off. His escape from the battlefield went unnoticed, such was the fury of the gunfire raging around the war wagon.

Rammakin was the first to go down, shot in the chest by a dozen rifle bullets. Gripped by total panic, Vance leapt off his horse and huddled behind a cluster of boulders. This was not what he had intended in joining up with the gang. He cowered behind the rocks, head down. Removing a grubby necker, he desperately waved it in surrender.

Meanwhile, the Kid was blasting away, a revolver in each hand.

The wagon driver clutched at his shoulder.

'Heehaw! Chew on that, dogbreath!' railed the crazed gunman continuing to fire wildly at anything that moved in the blurred pall of gunsmoke and dust. Another cry of pain from somewhere in the mirk brought another howl of delight from the sole remaining gunman.

These successes further roused the gunman's lust for blood. Hot lead flew past his ears, buzzing like angry hornets. But none found its mark. The Kid appeared to be leading a charmed life. Alternately, he cocked and fired the new Colt .45 together with the trusted old army Remington, blasting away until both hammers clicked on empty chambers.

'Aaaaaagh!' yelled the demented outlaw in frustration. Shucking the useless weapons, he grabbed for the rifle in its saddle boot. But he never managed to draw it. The sudden lull in the Kid's firing had given the hidden law officers the chance to zero in on their mark.

And they took full advantage.

Kid Branson's body was struck repeatedly by heavy rifle shells. The punctured torso was lifted from the saddle like an old discarded sock. Leaking blood from myriad wounds, it hit the ground with a dull thud and lay still.

Sudden quiet followed the brief but lethal exchange. The ears of the emerging lawmen rang from the recent drubbing they had received. Tillman was the first to jump down. Calculating eyes panned the scene of death, coming to rest on the bandanna waving from behind a rock.

'Come out of there, mister,' he rapped slowly advancing towards the hidden bushwacker. 'Throw your gun down. Any wrong move will be your last.'

The bare head of Eugene Vance rose above the rock. Both hands shook as they grabbed for a hunk of sky.

'D-don't s-shoot,' he stammered. 'I give up.'

'You bet your sweet mother you do,' growled the Socorro marshal as the rest of his borrowed officers quickly established that the downed outlaws had breathed their last. He turned to one of the men. 'Get the cuffs on this rat while I check out my buddy.'

Then Tillman hurried over to where Cal was struggling to get to his feet.

'You all right, partner?' he asked, worry lines etching the contours of his face.

Blood covered the left side of Cal's head. It trickled down from a three inch furrow and looked much

139

worse than it was; luckily, the silver conchoed lining of his hat band had deflected the full force of the bullet.

'Always pays to wear a good hat,' joked the injured man slumping to the ground. His breathing was firm but irregular, emerging in short bursts. He reached for the battered object lying in the dust and stuck a finger through the torn crown. 'Although I reckon a new one is gonna be needed.'

Tillman couldn't help laughing at his old pard's casual acceptance of his wound. Hurriedly he moved to support his back, dribbling water on to the parched lips. Then he untied his own bandanna and poured some of the precious liquid out, wiping away the bulk of the crimson veneer.

'Looks like you're gonna be with us for a spell longer.' A sigh of relief hissed through the set of grinning white teeth that beamed from beneath the thick moustache.

'Did we get Starkey?' inquired Cal, accepting the quirley that Tillman placed between his lips.

'He made a run for it soon as the shooting started,' replied Tillman. 'Nobody could follow him with all the bullets flying.'

Cal's head drooped when he realized that this part of the plan had gone wrong. 'So we're no nearer getting Cecelia back.'

'I wouldn't be too sure about that,' averred an upbeat Kansas Jack. 'Two of the others were gunned down but we captured Vance. The cowardly varmint hid behind a rock like a mangy cur. He's agreed to lead us to their camp.' The lawman shrugged. 'He wasn't given much choice. It was either that or a bullet in the back of the head.'

A gleam of hope was resurrected in the injured man's glassy eyes.

'Then what are we waiting for?' croaked Cal, attempting to struggle to his feet. 'Let's get moving.'

'Slow down there, partner,' chided Tillman catching him as his weakened legs gave way. 'First off, we need to get you back to town for some medical attention. A couple of days' rest and then we can go after him.'

Cal clutched his compadre's arm.

'But he'll have chance to get away before we can stop him. . . .' His face creased up in pain as a thousand hammers battered away inside his skull. Then he passed out.

'Over here, Roy,' Tillman called to one of the deputies. 'Help me get this stubborn critter into the wagon. And easy does it.'

'Who is this guy?' inquired the puzzled law officer as they carefully placed the injured man next to the chastened outlaw.

'Calls himself—' Tillman almost forgot that Lightning Cal Gentry was supposedly dead and buried. He speared Vance with a rabid look that promised an early grave should he reveal his buddy's true identity. 'Will Bennett. It's his wife that's been kidnapped.'

Although Doc Hobley recommended that his latest

patient needed to rest for at least a week, Cal insisted that he was fit enough to ride. Two days in bed had been more than enough to drive him to distraction.

'I can't force you to ease up,' sighed the medic, 'so if'n you have to go after this gang, take these.' Cal accepted the box of tiny pills. 'They've just arrived from back East. The claim is they help relieve headaches.'

'Much obliged, Doc,' said Cal mounting up. Beneath the Stetson, his head was swathed in a tight bandage.

Accompanied by Jack Tillman and a morose Eugene Vance, they jogged out of Safford heading north towards the broken canyonlands of the Natanes Plateau. Somewhere within the labyrinth of interconnected arroyos and gullies lay the hideout where Starkey would be holding Cecelia.

And Vance was the key to flushing him out.

Once it became apparent that he was more use to his captors alive than dead, the hardcase began making demands for his complicity. A free pardon and share of the bounties for the dead outlaws, just for starters. Tillman gave the claims due deliberation. Then he called a halt and gave his response in time-honoured fashion; a bruised and battered face attested to the efficacy of his persuasive methods.

In the meantime, Starkey had made good his getaway from the death-dealing scene at Warbonnet Rock arriving back at the hideout without incident.

The old bandit knew that Gentry had savings stashed away in the bank at El Paso even if he had surrendered the Nebraska haul. It might take longer to get the dough, but it would be worth it. And the jasper would pay anything to get his lady love back intact. She was his trump card for getting out of the territory in one piece.

Hidden away out here, nobody could find them except by pure accident. The odds against that happening were hundreds to one. He had enough supplies for a protracted sojourn and just needed to figure out how best to start up negotiations to secure the dough.

What he was unaware of was that the money had all gone to secure the ranch.

FOURTEEN

GERONIMO STEPS IN

The terrain north from Safford was initially quite lush: grassland ideal for beef cattle flourished in the Gila Valley and Herefords and Texas longhorns grazed contentedly on the rolling landscape under the early morning sun. But it was a narrow oasis that soon surrendered to rising foothills beyond.

Thereafter the trail entered the confines of dense pine forests snaking steadily upwards between steep-sided flanks. In consequence, the pace slowed to a stumbling walk. Only when they came to a broken stretch open to the sky was it possible to spur ahead.

As they moved higher, the tree cover faded but at the same time, the terrain became much rougher underfoot. Tillman soon noticed that Cal was lagging behind. He dropped back to see if his partner wanted to rest up for a spell. Vance now found himself taking the lead.

Swivelling in the saddle, his beady eyes quickly sensed that here was the ideal opportunity to make good his escape.

Vance chuckled to himself. His stocky frame tightened. Tillman had dropped back further, drawing level with the injured gunfighter. They were a good thirty yards back. And the lawman's attention was totally focused on assertaining the extent of Gentry's infirmity.

The arduous ride was taking more out of Gentry than he had reckoned with. And it would get worse as they neared the broken country of the Natanes.

Another ten yards and Vance judged that he could make his move.

He pulled ahead evenly with no sudden moves to forewarn his custodians as to any devious intent. They were coming to a bend in the trail. The outlaw held his breath praying they would not cotton to his stratagem. As soon as he was out of sight, the outlaw dug in his spurs. The horse lunged forward emerging into another broken stand of intermittent tree growth.

The sound of pounding hoofs instantly alerted the distracted lawman. Tillman cursed himself for being a stupid jackass.

'You stay here!' he shouted to the injured rider. 'Ain't no way you can chase after that crafty buzzard in your condition.'

Without waiting for a reply, Tillman unmercifully

leathered his own mount into motion. By this time, Vance was disappearing into the distance.

He had a good start, twisting this way and that amidst the irregular spacing of pine trees. Tillman knew that only an exceptionally lucky shot with a long rifle would bring him down. And if he reached the cover of the next thick stand of trees, the bastard might easily be impossible to flush out. All he would need to do was wait until nightfall, then sneek away.

Then they would never find the gang's hideout.

The lawman gritted his teeth. Head lowered to cut down wind resistance he doggedly urged his horse to full gallop.

'Come on, fella!' he yelled at the charging black stallion. 'Give me all you've got.'

The horse responded with a snorting whine and plunged forward lengthening its stride. Yet still the distance did not appear to be narrowing. And the next dense wall of dark green was only a half mile distant. Seeing his quarry escaping, the lawman drew his pistol and opened fire. But the distance was too great. It was an act of pure desperation.

However, the shots did not go unnoticed.

High up on a ridge overlooking the broad swathe of open woodland, a line of Apache warriors reined up their ponies. Like statues frozen in time, they remained still and silent, hooded eyes focused on to the strange pursuit unfolding below. Twenty braves carved from stone, bronzed faces daubed with streaks of yellow and blue, they maintained a watchful vigilance.

Their leader was a grizzled veteran of many forays against the blue coats. The grubby jacket he wore was a souvenir of one such incursion. On the right side of Geronimo sat his daughter Wind that Sings. They were heading north, back to their camp on the banks of the Bonito in the Maverick Heights.

The girl gripped her father's arm.

'That is man who helped me reach your camp,' she said, pointing at the rider who was about one hundred yards behind his quarry. 'I remember his red shirt and black leather vest. That Kansas Jack. And man he chase is one of bad men from Guthrie's Place.'

The Apache leader's wizened features resembled the cracked leather of an old moccasin. On hearing his daughter's declaration, the granite face hardened to an implacable determination. Here was the chance for vengeance.

Raising the Spencer rifle in his left hand, he jabbed it down the steep slope then plunged headlong over the rim. Unheeding of their safety, the braves followed.

Slithering and sliding down the loosely compacted shale, the descent set up a minor avalanche in its wake. Nor was it without casualties. One brave was swept from his horse by the protruding branch of a Joshua Tree. The horse of another failed to maintain its balance. Both man and beast were pitched headlong down the grade in a tangle of thrashing limbs.

Those who made it to the base of the stony gradient unharmed found that they were ahead of the

147

chase. Geronimo spread his braves across the trail to deny the fleeing outlaw any means of avoiding their welcome party. The steady drum of shod hoofs beating the ground grew to a thundering roar as the lead rider hove into view.

On witnessing this unexpected delay to his plans, the rider dragged hard on the reins to bring his snorting mount to a quivering halt. A look of stunned bewilderment faced the stoic line of braves. Quickly it turned to fear as Wind that Sings nudged her horse forward.

'This one of those who killed Little Dove,' she said in a flat tone.

'No!' hollered the terrified man. 'It weren't me. Jeb shot her.'

But the denial fell on deaf ears: his fate was sealed.

Geronimo jammed the Spencer into his shoulder and without preamble, pulled the trigger. Vance was lifted from the saddle, his left shoulder a ragged mess. But he still had enough strength to crawl away. Hope remained that somehow he might yet escape the retribution that was surely coming.

Wind that Sings stepped down. She signalled to one of the braves who nudged his mount forward and handed her a war lance decorated with eagle feathers.

'On your feet, white dog,' she snarled, hefting the deadly weapon as she slowly approached the quaking man. The Indians were mere observers, guardians to ensure that justice was carried through.

Vance hauled himself erect, his face ashen,

rubbery lips moving but incapable of verbalizing the terror that was eating at his heart.

'Now run!' ordered the girl. 'That more chance than sister given.'

Vance took to his heels – it was a stumbling gait more akin to that of a drunken cowpoke on a Saturday night. He managed to get ten feet before the lance was thrown. It pierced his back dead centre. The outlaw pitched forward on to his face. The attempted escape had reached its brutal conclusion.

The pursuing rider hurtled round a bend in the trail and also quickly came to a buffeting standstill. Nobody prevented him hurrying over to the outlaw and affirming that he was indeed past redemption.

Tillman's shoulders sagged. The gaunt features registered a despondent aura of gloom.

'You not pleased that bad man dead?' enquired a rather bemused Wind that Sings. 'Why you chase if not to catch and kill?'

Tillman threw his arms wide.

'Maybe that's on account of his being the only one who could have led us to the secret hideout where Starkey is holding my buddy's woman hostage.' The lawman couldn't contain the vexation irking his soul. 'Without him to lead us through the Natanes canyonlands, how can we possibly find her?'

He didn't expect a reply. But one came.

Geronimo pushed forward and locked his icy gaze on to the lawman. His face remained deadpan, unmoving, devoid of emotion.

'Maricopas!' The blunt summons brought another brave hustling to join his chief. 'You know every canyon in the Natanes, every bend in trail, every source of water.' It was a statement of fact that did not require a reply. The Apache brave known as Maricopas merely grunted an acknowledgement. 'You will pick up Starkey's trail and take us to his hideout.'

Tillman visibly relaxed, the colour returning to his pallid features. This was turning out better than he could have expected. Apaches were renowned scouts and trackers. And with Geronimo on their side, perhaps this caper would turn out right after all.

'I thank the great chief, Geronimo, for his help,' the lawman extolled his benefactor. 'Me and my partner are much indebted to you.'

'White man help daughter,' responded the Indian. 'Only right to repay.'

'Perhaps medicine man could help my partner.' Tillman had noticed that one of the braves sported the headdress of a tribal doctor. Some of their remedies were pure hogwash but others involving the use of herbs and animal potions were known to have surprising effects. Maybe this guy could invoke the spirits in Cal Gentry's favour. 'He has been injured and needs the attention of a worthy master to effect a cure.'

Mounting up, Indians and white man rode back down the trail to where Cal Gentry was resting.

FIFTEEN

BOXED IN

After examining the head wound, the medicine man known as Dull Knife gave an enlightened nod of the head. Displaying the practised ease reminiscent of a big city surgeon, he disappeared into a clump of vegetation. Nobody spoke while he was away.

Fifteen minutes later, Dull Knife returned clutching a handful of herbs and leaves. A brief flick of the hand and a brave stepped forward. The medicine man gave instructions for the molding of a compress to be applied to the wound. In addition, a special brew was heated over a fire. Its smoky preparation was accompanied by numerous chants and spells calling on the gods to ensure a successful result.

A look of scepticism passed between the two white men. The Indians sat round in a circle totally mesmerised by Dull Knife's swaying movements as he made ready to apply the physic.

'Drink!' ordered the medicine man handing a mug of vile smelling liquid to the patient. 'Make white man better before sun go down.'

Cal accepted the potion and drank it in a single gulp. The urge to vomit up the odious mixture was somehow contained.

There was no change in the patient's weakened state for some time.

But, as dusk phased out the sun's power, Cal did indeed begin to feel much improved. His strength was quickly returning. He was even able to polish off a hearty meal of fresh deer caught by one of the Indians.

'Dull Knife is fine doctor,' Cal praised the medicine man who accepted the lavish tribute with stoic disregard. His lined face did, however, hint at pleasure when Cal added, 'He should be made chief surgeon to Great White Father in the East.'

All the braves murmured their approval. Dull Knife basked in the glory.

Before the sun had crested the scalloped moulding of the ridge the next morning, the party was on the move.

Maricopas led the way.

It was a long hard ride through the never-ending maze of canyons that made the Natanes Plateau ressemble a giant spider's web. Each branch looked the same; this was not the place to enter without a guide. The gang must have had the luck of the Devil on their side to navigate their way across it.

Frequent halts were called while the tracker examined the ground. After carefully studying what had caught his attention, he pointed the way to proceed with confidence.

'He able to read land with special eye,' observed Geronimo according the brave's skill much deference. 'Lead us to hideout with no problem.'

It was early afternoon when Maricopas raised his hand.

The single file of riders drew to a halt.

Geronimo kneed his horse forward.

'Two horses come through here three moons back,' said the tracker pointing to a cluster of Juniper trees. 'They try to brush out tracks.'

Geronimo nodded as he caught sight of a boot heel and some broken twigs. Only a close-up survey had revealed the tell-tale signs. Maricopas had earned his feathers today.

'Look like end of trail,' said the tracker. 'I go through to make certain our enemy there. Chief wait here 'til I return.'

Effective delegation of authority and respect for the various talents of his men had made Geronimo a giant among the Chiricahua, and a thorn in the side of the military.

Maricopas was back within fifteen minutes.

He explained the situation beyond the tree cover, how a narrow ravine opened up to reveal an inner pasture with a cabin outside which two horses were tethered.

Jeb Starkey and Cecelia!

153

The two white men thanked their benefactors and assured Geronimo that they could handle the final showdown. The Apache was sceptical. He had hoped to avenge the death of his youngest daughter.

'We thank Geronimo and his brave warriors for their help. Without your intervention, Vance would have escaped and we might never have found this hidden canyon. Kansas Jack is US marshal.' Tillman's voice was flat. He tapped the tin star glinting in the bright sun. 'White killer should face white man's law. I will make certain that Starkey pays the price for his crimes,' he averred firmly. 'And if he escapes American justice, then Apache law can exact the full retribution as they think fit.'

The two men tensed, waiting for Geronimo's reaction.

The Apache chief sat his horse, unmoving, his face a blank mask. It was a long minute before he spoke.

'Geronimo agree.' The pair visibly relaxed. 'But Apache wait here until you return.' A flicker of a smile passed over the seamed façade. 'Make certain white eyes not lose bad fella again.'

Jeb Starkey was sitting at the table in the cabin shovelling a mixture of beans and fatback into his mouth. He poured out half a mug of coffee, topping it up from a bottle of whiskey. Cecelia eyed him morosely from the far side of the room. A hand gingerly felt the tender swelling on her cheek where Starkey had hit her following an abortive attempt to escape the previous day. She examined the bruise through a looking glass – it was turning yellow.

Initially the outlaw had allowed her a certain measure of freedom to move around at will. The cabin was well hidden and he was confident she could not get far without becoming lost amidst the broken terrain.

He was right. But that hadn't prevented the girl from trying. Now she was confined to the cabin at the end of a steel chain like a dog. She mouthed a curse at the surly figure.

Starkey caught the dour look aimed at him. He uttered a manic chuckle reading her colourful thoughts.

'Serves you right, girl,' he scoffed raising a hand to indicate more of the same should any further trouble be caused. 'And next time I won't be so lenient.'

'How long do you intend keeping me imprisoned in this hovel?' she cried. Her stiff resolve to maintain a proud bearing was rapidly breaking down. Tears ran down her dirt-streaked face.

Starkey afforded the query a pensive grunt. In truth he had no idea. Since reaching the hideout, he had come to the conclusion that this girl was more trouble than she was worth. And being stuck with her in this godforsaken wilderness was no darned picnic, that was for sure.

Maybe it was better just to cut his losses and head back to Kansas. He could leave the girl at a cross-roads in the Gila Valley. At least he still had his skin intact. Once he had quit the territory he could then look to set up a new gang. . . .

But he never got the chance to cogitate further on the dilemma. It was suddenly answered for him.

'You in the cabin!' called a brittle voice from outside. 'We have you surrounded. Come out with your hands raised and you won't get hurt.'

Black eyes wide and staring, Starkey leapt to his feet. He recognized that voice. And so did Cecelia.

'Cal, Cal!' she hollered, her words crackling with emotion. 'Thank the Lord you've come.'

'Let the girl go free, Jeb,' replied Gentry in a more even tone. 'You're penned in like a rat in a corner. Walk out or be carried. The choice is yours.'

Starkey wasted no time in idle speculation as to how the hideout had been discovered. Unlocking the chain, he grabbed hold of the girl and hustled over to the cabin door. Throwing it open, he emerged into daylight, a pistol jammed in the girl's ear. She was going to be his ticket to freedom. No way would his old partner in crime risk harming her.

'I'm riding out of here, Gentry,' he shouted. 'And the girl comes with me. I'll let her go when I know you ain't following. But not until then. Try anything funny, and she gets it.'

Cal had concealed himself behind a cottonwood on the edge of the clearing in front of the cabin.

'You all right, Cecelia?' he growled on witnessing the large bruise on her face. 'If that bastard's—'

'You gonna play ball, mister,' interjected the outlaw, 'or do I haul off here and now?'

At that moment his attention was attracted by a movement to his left. Swinging to face this new threat, he hugged the girl closer for protection against any skulduggery from this new quarter.

Tillman had sneaked around the edge of the clearing and slipped quietly along the wall hoping to catch the kidnapper unawares. The ruse might have been successful had his boot not connected with a pitchfork and given his position away.

Starkey recognized the lawman from past times.

'Well if'n it ain't Kansas Jack Tillman!' The exclamation of surprise was heavily laced with irony. His cocked revolver jabbed the girl's ear eliciting a yelp of pain which was ignored. 'And riding the Judas Trail I see.' His beady peepers flicked towards the tin star.

Tillman ignore the cutting reposte.

'You can't escape, Jeb,' he said. 'Best give up now while you got the chance. Cal ain't one to forgive and forget. Especially with his lady love sporting a shiner like that.'

'You said it, starpacker,' clucked Starkey. 'I'm dead meat whatever happens. So I might as well get hung for a sheep as a lamb.'

And with that he flung the girl against the lawman. Caught wrong-footed, both of them were upended, falling to the ground as the outlaw made good his escape round the far side of the cabin.

Witnessing the sudden fracas, Cal despatched a couple of shots towards the disappearing outlaw. The bullets chewed slivers of wood from the corner post. But Starkey was out of sight.

Glad that he had left his horse saddled, the outlaw

leapt astride and guided it through the dense thicket of trees behind the cabin where they abutted on to the soaring rock wall. Once clear of the cabin, he raced pell-mell for the head of the canyon.

Cal scuttled across the clearing. He took Cecilia in his arms and hugged her tightly. But this was no time for an emotive reunion.

'Take care of her,' he urged Tillman. 'I'm going after Starkey.'

He dashed back to his own mount and quickly set off in pursuit of the fleeing outlaw.

'Watch yourself,' Tillman called after his retreating back. 'That varmint is more slippery than a wriggling eel.'

A raised arm acknowledged the warning.

Twenty minutes of hard riding brought Jeb Starkey to the far end of what appeared to be a dead end. But he had investigated the box canyon on a previous visit for just such an eventuality as this. A narrow winding trail zig-zagged up the steep back wall. Unseen from below, it wound ever upwards between heavy mounds of fractured boulders.

Once he reached the rimrock, Starkey knew that he could disappear into the snarl of interlocking fissures that made up the huge jigsaw puzzle of the Natanes Plateau. Arriving at the bottom, Cal saw his nemesis disappearing up a ravine. Already he was near the crest. It would need a miracle now to catch up.

But that's what happened.

On struggling over the final lip of the canyon, the

outlaw's smile of triumph faded to a bleak awareness that his bid for freedom had been thwarted. His heart sank, a yawning gulf opening in his guts. The chance for a new beginning suddenly faded with the sun that slid behind a dark cloud.

Sitting their horses side by side, Geronimo and his Apache tracker were waiting. Suspecting that such a ploy would be attempted, they had ridden along the crest of the ridge leaving the others behind to keep watch on the hidden entrance to the canyon.

Starkey was given no opportunity to plead his case. A single bullet took him in the chest. Maricopas despatched three arrows into the slumping torso before it struck the ground.

'Apache law always best for Indian reprisal,' muttered Geronimo, the blank look displaying nary a hint of euphoria as he thumbed a fresh cartridge into the breech of the rifle; the tracker merely eyed the lifeless corpse with empty disdain. Then they began the slow descent into the box canyon.

Halfway up the tortuous trail, Cal ducked low in the saddle. The single throaty roar of a rifle echoed down the constricted ravine. At first he thought that the wily outlaw had spotted his pursuer and was trying to stop him. But the lethal strike of bullet on flesh or ricochetting against rock never came.

Then his head nodded in understanding. Sucking in a deep breath, he blazed forth with a yell of exultation realizing what had occurred high above him on the ridge. Dismounting, he lit up a cigar and waited for the two Indians to descend.

Once they had returned to the cabin, Cal hurried over to his waiting spouse. The strain of recent events showed in their drawn and jaded features but the final end to the horrendous drama tore down any reserve. Man and wife clung to each other like limpets; tears of joy flowed, unimpeded by the normal traditions of frontier reticence.

When at last they drew apart, Cal said, 'Perhaps now Lightning Cal Gentry can finally be put to rest in a deep grave, and we can make a new life for ourselves, Mrs . . . Bennett.'

Cecelia's pale features resolved into a joyous smile.

'I second that, Mr . . . Bennett.'